GLORY'S GROOM

THE ALPHABET MAIL-ORDER BRIDES BOOK 7

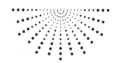

KATHLEEN BALL

*To the wonderful people in my Facebook Group- Kathleen Ball
Western Romance Readers, you encourage me every day.
Also to my wonderful mother-in-law Ginny Ball, I love you!
And as always to Bruce, Steven, Colt, Clara, Emery and Mavis
because I love them.*

CHAPTER ONE

"*N*ow you can all stop acting like you're surprised by my offer, considering how you girls all share secrets and everything else about your lives with each other." Madam Wigg waved her hand in front of her face as she looked around the room. "I'm quite certain it's old news around here already that my health is failing me and I'm making sure all of the foundling girls are given the chance to have a new life outside these walls."

Glory's heart sank. So it was true, they were all leaving. She'd so hoped that what they'd heard was just some strange joke but it wasn't. She glanced at her roommates, Imogene, Harriet and Fae. They were more like sisters to her.

They'd all discussed what had been going on at the school during their regular late night talks. The four of them shared two adjoining rooms at the school and had spent many hours over the years sharing secrets and talking into the wee hours of the morning.

Even though she knew deep down that this moment was coming she kept hoping it wouldn't and somehow she'd be spared. Madam Wigg already spoken to Abigail a few days ago, and Beulah had told them earlier today that Madam Wigg had come to her, Emmaline, Dorthy and Catalina with an offer too.

"It's no secret that my health is failing. I'd be doing you all a disservice if I let you stay here forever without even giving you the opportunity to see the world and to have the chance to spread the teachings of the Wigg School and Foundling Home to those who need it. I took you all in as babies, intending to give you the best life I could. And that's what I'm still trying to do, whether or not you believe me."

Now they'd have to leave the only home they'd ever known. Some girls were excited about starting new lives but not Glory. If she could stay forever, she'd be ever content.

Fae leaned forward in her chair, resting her arms on her legs. "But Wiggie, you don't look sick. I just find it hard to believe your health is failing."

"Fae, I know you always like to see the sunshine and rainbows in life, but that's not always how it works. Everyone dies. And at my age, it's best to be prepared."

Fae's brow furrowed. "You're not even that old."

Wiggie just shook her head and flapped her hand again. "Well, you can try telling that to these old bones." Wiggie looked at each one of them. "So, the offer is the same for you girls. Before I pop my clogs, I'd love nothing more than to see my teaching shared around the country. And, it would make me happy to see you all in charge of your own schools, content while leading the lives you deserve. Everyone needs the chance to explore life on their own, find someone who can love them the way my dear husband did, and to even have children of their own someday if they choose. That's what I'm offering you today."

Madam Wigg stared at Fae. "And don't you even try to tell me that isn't something you've always thought about in the back of your mind. I've seen the far-away looks, the moments you were lost daydreaming about some handsome gentleman who will sweep you off your feet like in those silly novels you read."

Fae's cheeks turned red as Glory, Harriet, and Imogene smiled. "You do daydream about it a lot, Fae," Imogene teased with a laugh.

Fae shot Imogene a look that sent the Imogene woman into another laughing fit.

"I will fund the school once you've got everything set up and ready. There are so many opportunities out west where the poor children aren't being given the chance for a proper education. I'm relying on you ladies to help me share my beliefs of inclusion and that everyone deserves the chance to learn."

"But, out west? It's so uncivilized." Harriet said. It was exactly what Glory was thinking. Harriet like herself didn't speak up much. Was Harriet as frightened to leave as Glory? There were too many unknowns out, on my, did she say the west? They were being sent into a place that had outlaws and Indians? It couldn't be true. She took a deep breath to keep from panicking. Surely Fae would tell Madam Wigg that they wouldn't go wouldn't she?

"And we'd be on our own. How could we manage without having each other to lean on? Who knows what could happen to us out there." Glory shuddered for extra emphasis.

Now would be the perfect time for Fae or Imogene to refuse. Glory waited but neither said a word. Her shoulders slumped. She was friends with all the women who taught in the school, but especially with Fae, Imogene and Harriet. She couldn't be without them.

"You'll all be fine. I'm not sending you out there all on your own. And don't pretend you don't know what I'm talking about. Everyone knows Abigail has been corresponding with a man out west and now the other women I've spoken to have started the process too. It's really the only way to afford to send you all out to these places before the money for the schools is sent to you. And don't worry that you'll be going out to marry a stranger who could be dangerous, or that you'll end up with some cantankerous old coot with no teeth of his own. I assure you, I'm going to be making sure every man you consider corresponding with is a suitable candidate and will personally do as much digging as I can to find out whether they are to be trusted or not." Wiggie looked around at the girls who were all staring at her dumbfounded. "What? You ladies all look like you'd never even considered the possibility of that happening. Well, no matter. Now that you do realize it could happen, you can rest assured knowing I'll make sure you choose the right men."

Wiggie struggled with her skirts as she tried to stand up. The old rocking chair that she sat in kept moving every time she did, causing the soft material to slip along the wooden seat. She muttered under her breath as she continued to struggle. Fae stood up and put her hand out for her to take.

"Thank you, dear. Now maybe you'll all believe me when I tell you this old body is just about plum worn out. I can't even get out of a chair on my own without looking like a half-dead fish flopping around on the ground." Wiggie stood up and brushed at her skirts. "Heavens, look at how wrinkled I am. I look like I've been rolling around wrestling with the children outside."

Fae laughed and shook her head. "Wiggie, you look exactly the same as you did when you walked in the door. You're just trying to make a fuss so we won't put up any more arguments and try to change your mind."

"Well, I'm leaving the idea here with you girls discuss. I know you will be as soon as I leave. I want you to at least consider it. I love you all like daughters, and I only want what is best for you. I hope you'll understand that while I've created this nest for you to grow in, it's time to spread your wings and share everything I've spent these years teaching you." Wiggie smiled at each of them. "And I have no doubt in my mind that each and every one of you will soar once you realize just what you're capable of doing outside the security of these walls."

There was silence when Wiggie left. What next? Look through ads from men who couldn't find wives? Maybe she should just close her eyes and point to one. Finally after much discussion with Fae, Harriet and Imogene, she picked one. The man who wrote the shortest ad; a man from Texas.

Wife needed at once on Texas Ranch. Please send inquiry.

A man without expectations.

———————

ALL TOO SOON IT was time to go. Glory put a brave face on but what she wanted was to hide in her special spot in the school where she went to be alone. It would be a long journey to Texas and she packed all her books about Botany. She knew so much about plants and cures. Perhaps she could be of some help in Texas. She'd studied up on plants that grew in the south and had put her knowledge in a handy notebook. She'd study and read more on the trip.

She didn't have much else to pack besides a few dresses that Fae had made for her. Things never mattered much. It was time to tell her goodbye to Madam Wigg, the only mother she'd ever known.

Glory swallowed hard as she entered the office. She was tongue-tied as always but Wiggie opened her arms and Glory hurried to her. None of the girls at the foundling home had been loved starved. Wiggie had always been there for them all. An impossible task some would say but Wiggie made it work.

"Glory, I'm not the least worried about you. You are a strong, capable woman even if you haven't realized it yet. You will blossom and I know good things will come your way. I wanted to tell you even though you picked the shortest advertisement; your husband to be was in the military and is highly regarded."

Glory drew back as her eyes widened. "How?"

"You must know by now I know everything that goes on with my girls. You have a gift for teaching and the school you end up at will be lucky to have you."

Tears filled Glory's eyes. "I've been the lucky one."

Wiggie gave her a gentle smile. "Come kiss me on the cheek before we both cry."

Glory kissed the older woman's cheek and Wiggie kissed her cheek in return.

"Remember, I love you and you are more than worthy of the love you'll find."

Glory nodded and almost tripped as she left. She said a few goodbyes, and it was all too much. Grabbing her bag she walked out of the Wigg School and Foundling Home and walked to the train station. She said one last goodbye to Wiggie and then she was soon joined by Harriet and Imogene. Fae was still saying her goodbyes. She'd always been outgoing. She joined them and they quickly formed a tight circle, their hands holding the ones next to them.

Glory laughed nervously, blinking her eyes hard as tears spilled out down her cheeks. "You're sure you have to go? I'd be willing to stay if the rest of you all were." Letting go of the hand she was holding, Fae pulled her into her arms. "Glory, we might not talk every day like we're used to, but we can all write to each other as much as we can. And maybe someday we can all get together for a visit."

Glory sniffed and wiped at her eyes when they pulled

apart. "I hope so. I don't know how I'll manage without all of you."

Fae swallowed hard against the lump that was forming. "You'll manage just fine, Glory. And you'll still have us. We're never more than a heartbeat away from each other."

"My train is leaving," Glory announced as she gave them each on last quick hug. She wished she had more time. A couple more years would have been just fine. She got on the train and immediately took her handkerchief out of her pocket. She managed to keep it damp for most of the trip.

CHAPTER TWO

*G*lory flew from her seat and ended up on the lap of a heavily bearded man who smelled ripe as the stage skidded to an abrupt stop. The man practically pushed her to the ground as he got up and made sure he was first out of the coach.

Gasping for air, she stood and tried to put her hat back on straight. Hopeless, she was hopeless. Her hair refused to stay pinned up. She must look; well there was no hope for it now. Smoothing down her skirt she saw fresh spit tobacco on it. Perhaps she could wipe the putrid stuff off with her hand-kerchief.

"Lady, I ain't got all day. I already unloaded your bag. Time for me to go."

Glory nodded and grabbed up her shawl, her reticule and put one white glove on. She'd lost the other one along the way. Her heart raced as she stepped down from the coach and almost ended sitting on her bottom in the middle of the dark dirt road. Where was the step? There was always a step for passengers to disembark easier.

A well-groomed man with black hair and kind blue eyes rescued her from a certain embarrassment.

"Thank you, kindly. I've always been clumsy but there wasn't a step."

The man stepped back and stared at her. He frowned slightly. If he frowned what would her groom think? The stage raced down the street and a rather large group of Union soldiers whistled at her. Glory quickly turned her back to them but it didn't stop them.

"Ma'am, might you be Miss Glory Wigg?" the dark-haired man asked.

She took a deep breath. "You must be Mr. Kent Sandler." Her body relaxed slightly, but she was still strung tight. He was clean and nice looking. She fretted the whole trip from New York City. At the beginning of the train trip there were mostly well groomed men with clean clothes on but the closer she got to Texas, a chill went up her back, the closer she got the worse the men smelled and acted.

"What happened?" Kent asked as he looked her up and down. "Did the stage tip over or something? Are you hurt?"

Smiling, she touched her hat. "No, this is the way I always look. Why do you ask?"

"Well, uh, never mind. The preacher is at the ranch waiting on us." He held out his arm and she hesitantly took it. "The wagon is just up ahead."

She halted practically pulling Kent back against her. "My bag! Where is my bag?" Letting go of Kent she hurried back to where she got off the coach. "The driver said he unloaded my bag." Her shoulders sagged.

"Was it a bag made of cloth with flowers on it?" he asked.

"Oh, yes! Where is it?" At the frown on his face her heart dropped.

"The man who got off ahead of you took it."

"Everything I owned was in that bag," she whispered. "It's best we get going. The preacher is waiting."

"I'm sorry if I had known it was yours…"

She took his offered arm and walked to the wagon with him. Eyeing it she didn't see any steps. How was one supposed to climb up onto this thing?

Before she could wonder more, Kent put his warm hands on her waist and lifted her up. She smiled down at him and furrowed her brow when he turned a bright shade of red. Making herself as comfortable as she could on the wooden bench, she waited for Kent to join her.

She never got to sit in the front of anything. Maybe Texas would be fun.

Kent sat down next to her, grabbed the lines and yelled, "Haw!"

The next thing she knew, she flew into the wagon bed with her skirts up around her thighs. "Ump!"

The wagon came to a sudden stop and then Kent climbed into the back of the wagon. "Are you all right?" He fixed her dress right off. Then he gently helped her to stand and lifted her back onto the seat. He sat next to her again. "I guess I forgot to tell you to hold on."

Her hat and most of her hairpins were in the wagon bed but at this point she didn't care. "I never rode in a wagon like this before. You couldn't have known."

"I am sorry. Hold on this time."

They were on their way. Should she laugh or cry? It was a choice she'd made often enough. This time she did neither. She swallowed hard and sat straight and tall as tall as one could while holding on.

"Why do you still have soldiers in your town? I heard all soldiers had left the south except for the most troublesome places." She scanned the area expecting to see an outlaw or two.

"Most towns still have soldiers. We stay mostly on the ranch."

"What animals do you have on the farm?"

He chuckled. "It's a ranch, and it's huge. It takes days to ride the whole perimeter. We mostly have cattle and horses. We have chickens."

"Do you ride the perimeter often?" She'd rather he'd stay near. He didn't know the soldiers were only in the dangerous towns.

"No, I mostly break horses. You'll like it there. Everyone is nice and helpful. We're like a big family."

The people of the foundling home and school had been her big family and look at what happened. One day you had a family and the next you didn't. Then you're pushed out to Texas and expected to put on a brave face and marry a man you didn't know. Her heart still ached for Imogene, Fae and Harriet.

"Sounds very nice, I can't wait to meet everyone." Hopefully she sounded as though she was excited.

They rode for about an hour when the houses and outbuildings came into view. "So much for first impressions," she murmured touching her hair.

"They won't care."

How she wished it was so but she knew better.

KENT REINED in the horses and set the brake tying the lines around the brake. He certainly got lucky. Glory was a pretty girl with her long brown hair that seemed to be full of curls. Her blue eyes were expressive, and she was easy to read. Her skin was so fair as though it had seen little sun.

He grinned as he hopped down from the wagon and rounded the wagon to help his bride. She was still fussing at her hair. It didn't matter to him but it appeared to matter a great deal to her.

He put his hands around her small waist and lifted her down. "Don't worry. No one here expects perfection." She looked into his eyes and gave him a smile that didn't fool him.

Offering her his arm, he waited until she put her small hand in the crook of his elbow and then walked toward the ranch owner Parker Eastman's house. It honored him his friends were waiting to meet her. They walked up the steps and Kent shook Parker's hand.

"This is Glory."

Parker smiled at her warmly. "Welcome. We've been as excited as Kent here for your arrival."

"Th-thank you."

Georgie, Parker's lovely wife stepped forward. She took Glory's hand. "Traveling mishaps? Don't worry we've all been there. Veronica, Sondra let's get Glory ready for the wedding. Kent, grab her bag will you?"

"All she has is her reticule. Her bag was filched in town," Kent explained.

"Oh you poor dear, I came with nothing but rags. It was too expensive for me to buy material at the time. Come, I know just the dress for you to wear." Georgie gestured for Glory to go in first and Veronica and Sondra followed them.

"I might as well go get ready," Kent said. He was feeling nervous; marriage was forever.

"We'll join you won't we?" Parker asked the other men.

Max smiled widely. "I bet we can give him some advice," he teased.

Once they were all at Sandler's new house, he braced himself for the ribbing he was bound to get.

"What happened to her? It looks like she was horsed dragged," Walter Green said.

They had all served together in the army. Parker Eastman had been their Captain. Austin Maxwell was a sergeant. Lex Willis and Walter Green were corporals like himself.

"Walter, you don't say that to the groom," Parker admonished.

"Well, what happened then?" Walter asked.

"She arrived rumpled and then she didn't know to hold on to the wagon and she went flying hard into the back of it." The men all laughed loudly and Kent joined them. Then he sobered.

"She has nothing to change into and she's self-conscious." Kent stared each of them in the eyes one by one. "Everyone better act like she is the loveliest bride you've ever seen." He stared at Walter the longest.

Kent changed his clothes. He'd bought his first suit a week ago. "How Do I Look?"

"Like Kent Sandler in a suit," Max replied.

Kent looked up to the ceiling. "God, give me patience and keep me from having to punch anyone today."

Parker slapped him on the shoulder. "Let's get out there, the preacher is waiting and don't worry I'll keep these two in line. The cowboys know better."

"Anyone from Joy coming?" Kent asked.

Joy was a place on the ranch where Parker had built houses for the ex-slaves. He'd given them paying jobs and everyone on the ranch pitched in to keep them safe from the men who rode at night wearing hoods, wreaking havoc against the freedmen.

"I invited them," Willis told him. "Let's go."

Kent's stomach soured as he and Parker walked to the front of the crowd and stood with the preacher. Maybe he should just give her to Willis, and then Willis could have the new house. The bunk house wasn't that bad. Darn Parker for making a bet that the first to marry gets a house. Max was the first and he and Veronica, his mail-order bride, seemed thrilled. Kent thought to be the end of wife hunting but Parker made the same offer to Kent and Willis. Why did Willis have to be so darn competitive? Kent never wanted to be married again.

Parker elbowed him. "No frowning. Here she comes."

Kent's heart thumped hard and fast against his chest. He'd known she was pretty, but she now was so exquisite. The word perfection came to mind. Their gazes met and held as she walked down the aisle to him. She gave him a shy smile when she stood next to him.

Georgie hurried through the crowd and stood at Glory's side breathing hard as though she'd lost her breath.

Kent couldn't stop staring at Glory. Her neck was long and graceful and he couldn't wait to kiss her there. First, he'd start at her rosy lips. These were probably not the appropriate thoughts to have standing in front of a preacher. She seemed nervous. She kept shifting from one foot to the other. This was bound to be a huge change for her. Did he have it in him to treat her gently?

Her eyes sparkled when he placed the ring on her finger. She looked to be in awe.

"I now pronounce you man and wife!" the preacher announced. "You may kiss the bride."

Kent froze for a second before he leaned down and brushed his lips against hers. He took her hand and gave it a light squeeze. He felt triumphant when she squeezed his hand back.

"You look beautiful. That green dress is beautiful on you," he whispered as they walked back down the aisle. "I heard the women made plenty of food and Veronica made a wedding cake. I know it must be hard for you to be away from home."

She nodded. "I miss my friends Fae, Harriet and Imogene

so much but I imagine they are all going through the same thing. They were and still are my family but I also have a new family now; I have you. I will try my very best to be the best wife ever."

He pulled her into an embrace and kissed her on the cheek. "I know you will."

"This ring is so very gorgeous but it's too expensive for a mere orphan who doesn't know where she came from."

"You're my wife now and I want you to wear the ring. It was my mother's, and she gave it to me before I went off to fight the war."

Her genuine smile of deep happiness had him smiling in return. Maybe this time he could love his wife.

People had congratulated them when a buggy came quickly up the road to the house. It stopped in a flurry of dust. Kent groaned in an ill-fated surprise. It was his mother-in-law, Sharon. He'd secretly thought of her as the witch.

Kent let go of Glory. "I'll be right back." He hurried to the buggy. Sharon had her usual scowl on her face and she held a wriggly child.

"Getting married again? Good luck to the poor woman you conned into marry you this time." Her voice was loud enough for everyone to hear.

"What do you want?"

"You never came home after you left the army. You never once checked on me!"

Kent frowned. "Why would I? The scathing letter you sent after Tammy's death was more than enough."

Sharon held the child out to him. "Here this heathen is yours." She dangled the boy until Kent took him into his arms.

"Why didn't you tell me? How could this child be mine?"

Her grin was sickening. "Oh, remember you came home right before the end of your time in the army? Tammy got you nice and drunk and then nine months later she died having your baby. I didn't tell you. I wanted to punish you but I think trying to raise this horrible boy is punishment enough." She motioned for the driver to drive away. She threw out a suitcase onto the drive and Kent watched as it bounced and rolled before it came to a stop.

The pain his dead wife had caused through their marriage hit him all at once and he felt the need to be alone but that wasn't possible. His happiness that had been so abundant moments before was now replaced with loathing and despair. He doubted the child was even his. He remembered nothing from that visit to see her except for her harping and he woke up hung over. But since they'd been married he was legally the father.

Glory rushed to his side and took the bewildered child from him. She crooned to the child, and he wrapped his arms around her neck.

———

"Could someone go get his suitcase? We don't even know his name," Glory called out to the crowd. She turned to Kent. "You don't know his name right?"

Veronica came to her side. "I'll take him and see he gets something to eat." Glory smiled her thanks, but the boy refused to let go of Glory.

"It's fine. He's scared. I remember from the orphanage when we'd get a young child, how frightened the young one was. Mostly the orphanage only took in baby girls but occasionally there would be an exception."

"Kent how long ago did you see your wife?" Glory was trying not to dwell on the fact he'd had a first wife.

"Almost three years ago I suppose. She found out we were in Texas and wrote a letter indicating she was on death's door. Captain Eastman, Parker, let me go home. She was fine she missed me."

"Here comes Crumb with the suitcase. Maybe there is information in it," Kent said his voice devoid of emotion.

Why the cowboy's name was Crumb Glory wanted to ask, but she found herself tongue-tied again.

"Come, let's go inside our house," Parker said as he took the suitcase from Crumb.

Glory walked with the child. She looked back and there stood her husband looking so lost it hurt her heart.

"Don't worry I'll get him," Parker told her.

Everyone stared at her and she couldn't get into the house fast enough. Crowds made her nervous. She'd always been more of a loner.

Georgie showed her where to sit. It was a comfortable chair. It was the most comfortable chair she'd ever sat upon. "Let go sweet boy and I'll hold you in my lap. Don't be afraid."

He slowly released the grasp he had around her neck and sat on her lap putting his cheek against her chest.

Georgie brought him a cookie and some milk but he wasn't interested. The two women exchanged worried glances and when Kent and Parker entered the house the boy turned his face away from them and whimpered.

All Glory could do was to rock him back and forth. It had always calmed the small children at the foundling home. What were Fae, Imogene and Harriet doing right now? She hoped with all her heart they had found good men and loving homes. It would have taken her longer to get to her destination so they could all be married by now.

Parker carried the coffeepot to the table in front of the sofa and Kent was right behind with the cups. Parker poured the coffee while Kent handed them out. He set Glory's on the table. His brow furrowed as he gazed into her eyes.

Another woman might have been upset but to Glory each child was a blessing. She bestowed what she hoped was her most understanding smile on Kent. "He's a beautiful child. I have one concern; If he's two why hasn't he uttered a word?"

Georgie picked up her own infant and held him as he cooed. "Perhaps the trip was hectic? Maybe he was attached to that horror of a woman, what was her name?"

"Sharon," Kent muttered as he frowned. "I don't understand the why. Why didn't they tell me I had a son? I would have gone back and raised him. I let him down before I even knew about him." A pained expression flashed across his face.

"You would have," Parker reassured him. He took a sip of coffee and cocked his left brow as he stared at Georgie.

Kent stood and grabbed the suitcase. He rummaged through it and mumbled under his breath. He turned back to them and shook his head. "Just odds and ends, mostly diapers. There's a towel, a sleeping gown and this piece of paper. It reads, *Tell Kent I hated him from the start.* I suppose that was from my wife, Tammy."

Glory wished she could put her arms around Kent to provide him with comfort. He looked so alone.

"What will you name him?" she asked Kent.

"Let's name him Theodore after my Grandfather. We'll call him Teddy. Do you think he'll let me hold him?"

Glory was sure Teddy would put up a fussy, but she gently lifted him from her lap and carried him to Kent. She set the boy in Kent's arms and instantly Teddy wailed at the top of his lungs. Immediately Douglas, Georgie's baby cried too.

Glory didn't immediately take Teddy into her arms. He'd have to get used to his father, bit by bit. After a minute she held her arms out, and he practically jumped into them. Then he was eerily silent.

Parker chuckled. "Don't worry about it, Sandler. Kids are like that. Tomorrow, you and Max can go into town and get things for your charming wife and handsome son. Max made the same trip when Georgie arrived and then again when Veronica and Bridey came. He knows what to buy. Glory, check and see if you need anything else. We have coffee, flour, sugar, and the like in a storage shed so help yourself. Now you three go and see your new home.

CHAPTER THREE

*K*ent was emotionally spent, but he opened the door to the house and lifted both Glory and Teddy into his arms and carried them over the threshold. Her surprised smile soothed his battered heart. Carefully he set her back on her feet and then he gently touched the top of Teddy's head. He had to admit the boy had his coloring; brown hair with blue eyes. Still Kent had his doubts. Tammy had played him for a fool one time too many.

He leaned in and kissed Glory's cheek. "Thank you for not running away when Sharon arrived. I'm glad Teddy is so taken with you." Then he grinned. "I have a feeling we might have to wait to have our wedding night."

Her resulting blush delighted him. He never gave it much thought but being from the Wigg Foundling home and School and trained to be a teacher he knew her to be an innocent, untouched woman. He'd never really known such goodness before in any woman he'd been interested in. He'd thought Tammy was… Tammy wasn't anything she led him to believe.

Glory was already going from room to room looking at

the house. She glanced at him over her shoulder and smiled. Her smile filled him with hope.

"I take it you like it."

"Like it? Oh my, I didn't expect anything so nice out in the wilds of Texas." She walked into the kitchen.

His lips twitched. *The wilds of Texas?* They were actually among the most civilized. She seemed nice enough though shy, and she was pretty to look at.

He heard banging, and he walked into the kitchen. Teddy was on the floor with a wooden spoon hitting the floor.

"I hope you don't mind. Lots of things can become toys. He crawls, but he doesn't walk. I know doctors cost a lot but I'd feel better if they checked Teddy over." She bit her bottom lip as she gazed at him.

"I'll see what I can do while I'm in town. You sew don't you?"

She stared at the floor for a moment before answering. "They teach all of those things at the orphanage."

"I'll get material for both you and the baby. After we eat, I'll ask Georgie if she has an extra cradle."

"He might be too big for a cradle," she commented.

"They have a couple out in the barn that might be of different sizes. I'll ask."

"Look at all the food we have. I won't have to cook for a week!" There was that smile again.

"Good, let's eat. I want to get to work on the cradle. Do you need any help?"

"As long as Teddy is content I can do it. Will chicken and potato salad be fine with you?"

"Wonderful." Kent sat at the table and watched his son. *His son* it was so strange to find out he was a father. That was on Sharon for sending him the telegram that his wife was dead with no mention of a child.

The note in the suitcase puzzled him. He thought they'd

been happy at first. Her constant flirting and need to be the center of attention became a problem. Other women in town had whispered about her, so he stopped taking Tammy to barn dances and picnics. She turned so sour after that. She wouldn't allow him to touch her and then he was conscripted to the Army.

He'd written her plenty, but she never replied until she got a message to Parker that they needed Kent at home. She probably found herself pregnant and had to make it look like it was his. It angered him she was a liar, and he was so gullible. Now it didn't matter. Children were innocents and shouldn't have to endure their parents' actions.

Glory set the food on the table then she picked up Teddy and sat him on her lap. He instantly lunged for everything except for the food. He was so quick he almost got her knife. She took a small piece of chicken and held it to him. "Are you hungry?"

He scrunched up his forehead, but he didn't answer. He pushed her hand away.

"Kent, when you go to Georgie's can you ask for some milk? Or is there a cow?" She stood with Teddy in her arms and looked on the shelves. "How about some porridge? Kids always like porridge."

"I'll get you milk. You need to eat, Glory."

"I am hungry. Would you like to hold him again?"

He braced himself for some screaming but as soon as Glory put Teddy in his arms he quietly stared up at him. Teddy's eyes were the same shade of blue as his. The boy grabbed at the buttons on Kent's shirt then they moved on to the shirt collar. Then he pulled lightly at Kent's lower lip.

Kent winked at Glory right before he howled in pain. Teddy had both of Kent's ears in his hands and he was pulling on them with all his might. "Teddy, let go."

Teddy smiled and pulled harder while he tried to get his mouth on one.

Glory hopped up and gently pried Teddy's little hands off of her husband's ears. It was obvious by the merriment in her eyes she was trying not to laugh. Finally, she succeeded.

She took him into her arms. "You little dickens, you." She rubbed his back, and he immediately put his head on her shoulder.

Kent touched both of his ears to make sure they weren't bleeding. "I'd best go get that milk now and ask about the cradle." He stood rubbing his right ears. Teddy had a strong grip.

GLORY YAWNED. What a long day! She was used to the structure and routine of the orphanage and school. It had been nothing but utter chaos all day. She still had to feed Teddy and get him to bed. Kent said they would postpone the wedding night, and she hoped he'd keep to that. Marriage sounded nice except that part. She didn't know much about the whole subject. Did they talk about it at school?

Perhaps she should have paid attention more. All she wanted to do was find plants that helped to heal. It fascinated her. You could grind up one plant add a pinch of another plant and it could help someone. The biggest losses were the notes and drawings of each plant. She read everything about the art of healing she could find.

Sometimes she'd hide in her spot and read. There was a window seat in a storage room no one used. She'd found it early on when she was just a child and little by little she'd made it hers. She'd sewn pillows to make it more comfortable. The crooked seams Glory had sewn had horrified Madam Wigg.

Glory smiled. Madam Wigg had frowned at Glory's first attempt and kindly told her to try again. Glory tried again. Madam Wigg asked her who had taught her to sew. When Glory told her it was her, her mentor's eyes grew wide. Madam Wigg wasn't one for punishment but Glory wasn't to go to supper until she sewed a straight seam.

While everyone left to eat, Glory's friend Fae snuck back in and quickly sewed the seam for her. Glory missed her and all the girls. She had a lot of good memories though.

It was dark outside and Glory's nerves tightened. Normally she didn't talk much to people. In fact, if she was invisible it would suit her fine. Fae, and Imogene did enough talking, and she rarely had to talk to a stranger. She never knew what to say, certain she'd say the wrong thing.

So far today she'd done well meeting her husband and the others on the ranch. Hopefully she'll be able to keep to herself much of the time.

The door opened. "I got milk but no cradle." Kent set the milk on the table.

"Teddy is almost asleep but I don't think we should let him sleep without eating. He will wake up in the middle of the night screaming. I'd just as soon make the porridge now then later. What do you think?"

"It makes sense. I know little about children. There are some on the ranch but I say howdy. I hold Parker's little one occasionally and Veronica and Max have little Bridey. Cradles do tend to be the same size."

She handed Teddy to Kent who looked a bit wary.

"Now no pulling my ears this time," he told his son.

She laughed as began the porridge.

"Georgie agrees with you about the doctor."

"Oh? Good." He obviously didn't have any confidence in her. It was fine she supposed. She had no confidence in herself either.

When the porridge was cooked and then cooled she put some in a small bowl. "Do you want to feed him or would you rather I do it?"

"I think he'd eat sitting on your lap better," Kent said. He stood and waited for Glory to sit. He then handed her the quiet child.

Teddy ate the first spoonful and smiled. It was a relief. She put the second spoonful in his mouth and instead of swallowing it he spit it out all over her. Glory could feel it in her hair.

"You need to swallow it, Teddy." She tried again, and he ate until it was all gone. He even had a bit of milk.

Kent's gaze was upon her and she didn't enjoy the merriment in his eyes. Well, he'd seen her at her worst and he hadn't run. It's a good sign.

"I will clean up here. Can you get Teddy ready for bed?"

"I have a better idea. Why don't I clean the dishes and bring you in some warm water so you can get the food out of your hair? Did you know if you leave porridge overnight it hardens and it's near impossible to get off?"

"I'm well aware of it. I'd be happy to change you, Little Teddy," she kissed his cheek. She stood and turned. "Thank you, Kent. I've heard many men don't help their wives and well, I appreciate it." She hurried into the bedroom.

———

KENT GRINNED AS SOON as the door was shut. She seemed a mite nervous. He'll go in after a while. He wanted to be sure she was changed into her nightgown. He had no intention of bedding her. Glory certainly knew what to do with a child and he was thankful.

He became a husband and a father all in one day. How

would it all play out? Would they get along together? He sure hoped so.

Tammy left him a mess. He knew when she didn't write back to him she was stepping out on him. It was easy to guess. He didn't know what he'd done to make her hate him. He'd put a stop to her outrageous teasing of any man she came across. She'd become an embarrassment, and he didn't like the looks he got whenever he was in town.

As far as he knew she hadn't strayed, but they'd been together such a short time before he was called up to join the army. Her hidden meanness had come out then. She lit into him saying he wasn't a good husband, provider or lover. She laughed at his confusion and taunted him even more. By the time he had to go he was eager to get away from her.

Poor Teddy, it was strange that he didn't talk or walk. He seemed bright eyed and alert. They had a new doctor in town. The last doctor liked his whiskey better than his patients. Kent would ask Max if he could get clothes for Glory and for Teddy and then summon the doctor. His heart pained him trying to imagine what happened to Teddy. Whatever was the matter, Kent would help his son in any way he could. Poor little boy, Kent was all he had. He had Glory too.

At least she could ease into her new role as mother and wife. There was so much food she wouldn't need to cook for a while. Since they didn't have many clothes, the washing should go quickly. Did he ask her if she could ride? She'd need to know how to shoot too.

The section of the ranch Parker had allowed the freedmen to build on, as long as they worked for him, was growing. The houses were well built and Parker had made sure they wouldn't need to go into Spring Water. He was afraid they'd be strung up if they did.

Tensions were building but the men of Eastman ranch

had shown the Ku Klux Klan that they could protect the ranch against them. There were plenty of guesses who these men were but they could substantiate none.

He stretched his arms overhead. Long day! He got up and walked to the closed door. He put his ear against it trying to figure if Glory had gone to bed already. There wasn't a sound, so he opened the door.

Teddy lay sleeping in the bed's middle while Glory was awake with a pinched look on her face. She held the sheet up to her chin and watched him with big eyes.

He nodded. "I'm going to get undressed if you want to look away."

She quickly turned away, and he smiled. He could see the redness of her blush on her neck and cheek. He didn't wear pajamas, he just wore his underwear. He took off his pants and shirt and socks and climbed in next to his son.

He turned on his side facing them and was warmed by the smile Glory gave him when she turned toward him.

"Relieved?" he asked as he cocked a brow.

"Yes, I'm relieved that the day is finally over. Tomorrow will be a better day," she whispered back.

She missed the point. She was as innocent as they come. "We won't be able to have our wedding night for a few days at least," he said in a low voice.

Glory swallowed hard and nodded. "Thank you for all of your thoughtfulness today. I'm thinking another man wouldn't have had the patience for me."

He leaned inward. He'd just been himself. There were probably some men who would have been put off by her clumsiness. "It's me who should thank you. You didn't have to immediately take to Teddy. You took both of us in stride and showed great kindness. I'm glad I ended up with you as my wife."

Her smile was radiant. "You sure are a charmer. Good

night, Kent." She snuggled into her pillow and closed her eyes.

"Good night," he whispered.

HE'D THOUGHT it would be a peaceful night, but he was dead wrong. Teddy cried out in his sleep as he thrashed around hitting them both. Glory jumped out of bed with a stunned look on her face.

"Teddy, wake up," Kent said. He said it again only louder.

When Teddy didn't open his eyes, Glory sat on the bed and pulled Teddy onto her lap and wrapped her arms around him. "It's all right. You're safe here with your father and me." She continued to croon to him until he settled down and fell back into a peaceful sleep.

Her gaze met Kent's and he could see how upsetting it had been for her.

"I sometimes have nightmares from my time in the Army. It scares me to think of what his nightmares are about," he confessed.

Her forehead wrinkled. "Was it so terrible? I mean being in New York City in the orphanage, things didn't change much for us. We didn't have a family to lose."

"We saw things no person should ever have to see. Most of us lost our families and land. Some of our soldiers didn't have shoes or coats. We had to take what we could from our dead friends so we could survive. I dream about battles and how people died and were wounded." He closed his eyes. He hated remembering it all.

"Did you get injured?"

He frowned. "I have scars." He didn't want to talk about it.

She gazed at him in the moonlit room and nodded. "Good night then."

He turned so his back was facing her and Teddy. His leg

acted up. He hated to look at it and he didn't know how he'd allow himself to let Glory see it. He'd have to have the lights off if they ever got a wedding night. He wouldn't want to scare her.

Finally he drifted off.

CHAPTER FOUR

he next morning it was decided that Max would go into town alone. Glory caught up to him and asked him if he could find a few small toys for Teddy. Max smiled and agreed.

That had been almost four hours ago. Kent was outside working with the horses while she checked the front window every few minutes for the doctor. She'd already made bread and cookies. She only knew how to cook those two items. Thankfully, there was plenty of food left over from the wedding. She'd have a few days yet before she'd have to confess her inadequacy as a wife. It would horrify madam Wigg if she knew just how many thing Glory failed to learn.

She was looking forward to walking the woods and seeing what plants and roots she could find to make healing powders, plasters and tinctures. She was good at that. It was upsetting to have lost her book of healing but she knew most by heart.

She'd given Teddy a wooden spoon and a wooden bowl to play with. He enjoyed the loud noise it made. She'd gotten on the floor and tried to show him how to crawl. He laughed and clapped his hands. It was probably hard to see what she was doing with her skirt and petticoats on.

Finally she heard horses and the unoiled springs of a buggy outside. She peeked out the window, and it looked to be the doctor. She watched as Kent quickly crossed the yard and shook the doctor's hand. They spoke briefly and turned toward the house. She quickly stepped away from the window, not wanting them to know she'd been watching.

She smiled when the door opened and happily greeted the doctor.

"So this is the boy?" he asked looking at Teddy.

"Yes, Dr. Bennett. We know nothing about him," Kent answered.

"I'll examine the child and see."

She observed as the doctor made friends with Teddy by giving him a wolf whittled out of wood. Teddy immediately warmed up to him. Next he was able to get Teddy to sit on the kitchen table while he looked him over.

The doctor stood behind Teddy and clapped his hands and seemed pleased when Teddy turned toward him.

"He's not deaf. The back of his head is flat. It is my opinion that he'd been left to lie in his cradle or crib with no one picking him up, for great lengths of time. I think no one interacted with him. They fed him, changed him but they probably never talked to him."

Kent took her hand in his. "What does all that mean, doctor?"

"In my opinion, Teddy has a lot of catching up to do but eventually he'll be running, playing and talking by school age. It'll take patience on your part. Sometimes when we perceive a child to be as old as Teddy we have certain expectations. He might benefit from interacting with Parker's son. Keep a good watch on him. He's much bigger than Douglas and could hurt him. Douglas just learned to crawl and is mumbling getting ready to talk. Kids learn quickly and I don't see any reason Teddy shouldn't. He also seems underweight."

He turned to her. "Good meals with vegetables and meat would be what he needs. You might need to chop everything into tiny pieces at first. Oh, and plenty of milk too." He set Teddy back on the floor and took Glory's hand. "Take it slow and it'll be worth it."

"Thank you, Dr. Bennett. You've eased my mind greatly."

Dr. Bennett grabbed his bag and placed his hand on Kent's shoulder before he left. "I'm optimistic, Kent."

Kent went outside with the doctor, probably to pay him.

She sighed and tears fell. Quickly she wiped them away. How cruel to leave a child in a crib. She could only imagine how much he cried, and no one came to see what was wrong. Perhaps he learned to be quiet. If Sharon was here, she'd strike her.

Glory sat on the floor and took Teddy into her arms and then set him on her lap. She felt the back of his head. It was flat. Her stomach churned. She hummed and rock the little boy and he turned his head and smiled at her.

Kent came back in and he smiled as he watched them. "I'm just so grateful. I didn't know what to think."

"I feel the same way. His head is flat on the back. How cruel that Sharon must have been. I think if we keep working with him, it'll be fine."

"You sure know what to do with a child."

"It was one thing I was good at. I tried to connect with the new orphans. It's rewarding to see them come out of their shells. I would have spent all my time with the little ones if I could. Madam Wigg expected all of us to have a well-rounded education so we could maintain a house and teach others."

He squatted down and kissed Teddy on the head, and then he kissed her cheek. He looked into her eyes and smiled. "That reminds me. Georgie wants to open a school for the children of the freedmen. I don't know if you have any interest in teaching them. I don't know if you interacted with people of different races at the orphanage but I only want you to do it if you feel you can feel kindly toward them. If you say no, I won't judge you."

"I'd love to. And you're right; children can feel if someone pretends to like them. They wouldn't trust that person and they wouldn't end up learning much. I've been around many people. I never knew why some groups of people were considered inferior."

Kent put his hands on her cheeks and turned her head enough he could kiss her on the lips.

It was a wonderful kiss that started so slow and ended up burning fires inside her. When he pulled away, it dazed her.

He stood and grinned. "I have to get back to work. I'll let Georgie know about the school."

Her heart felt lighter than it had since arriving in Texas. It would be an honor to teach children who hadn't had access to an education before. She knew the freedmen lived on the ranch in an area they call Joy. It would probably be a good idea to introduce herself to the children and get an idea of what they needed.

On the way down from New York she'd heard school books were hard to find in Texas since they were printed in the North. She could write to the orphanage and see if they could send something. She had the money for a school and hopefully all the supplies.

"Teddy how would you like to take a walk with me? We'll meet new people." Her heart skipped a beat. New people? More new people? Sometimes her shyness overwhelmed her. She paced back and forth and concluded she had no other choice. If she wanted the school she needed to meet the students.

Scooping up Teddy she went outside and walked down the hill to Joy. It wasn't far from her home. There looked to be about twenty well-built houses. Ten on each side of the road facing the house across from it. Children played in the dirt road and women were hanging laundry, churning butter and sewing. It felt very calming.

As soon as she stepped onto their road, everyone went into their houses and shut the door. She furrowed her brow. Why would they do that? She stopped at the first house on the right and knocked. No one answered, and she knew people were in there. Her shoulders slumped as she walked to the next house and the next. No one answered.

She got to the end of the street and knocked on the last house on the right side. The door opened surprising Glory. The woman was petite with dark skin, hair and eyes. There were three little ones hanging on her skirt.

"Well, what is it? You've already knocked and knocked on people's door. Where are from?"

"I married Kent Sandler." She shifted Teddy to the other hip and realized that the dress she wore, her only dress was horribly wrinkled and stained. "Forgive my appearance. I only have the one dress for now."

The woman stared at her.

"I grew up in an orphanage and was trained to teach. I would like to be your teacher if that would be acceptable to you. Everyone would have a say. I wanted to introduce myself and see if schooling was important. I know in some places they'd rather the children help out at home. I—"

"You certainly do talk a lot." She gestured to a bench right outside her house. "Let's sit a spell. I'm Letty and these three children are mine. Hannah is eight years old. Daryl is seven and Betsy is six. We ain't had no learning, but I prayed that we could get some. Darrius told me no one wanted us educated. But I kept prayin'."

"It's nice to meet all of you. I'm Glory Sandler. Oh, and this is Teddy."

Letty cocked her head to the side. "What's wrong with him? Don't his legs work?"

"My husband didn't know he had a child. His first wife died, and no one told him. They dropped Teddy off yesterday."

"Left him to rot," Letty said as she touched the back of his head. "Not your husband. Whoever's been taking care of him. He'll be fine. I've seen this before when the masters thought tending to the crop was more important than tending to a baby. You just keep talking to him and letting him watch you and he'll start walking in no time. See his eyes? They are nice and bright. That means he has some smarts."

"Thank you for your words of wisdom, Letty."

Letty laughed. "Imagine that, I have wisdom. So when does this school start and where is it?"

"Well, I have to talk to Mrs. Eastman but I do know they've been planning to build a school on the ranch. I haven't actually ever taught before but I have the necessary training." If they didn't expect her to teach cooking and sewing, she'd be fine. "What do you think? Is it a good idea and should I try to get the school built?"

"Will you teach the adults too? I want to read so bad." Letty's voice touched Glory's heart.

"I'm from the North. Is it true you weren't allowed to learn to read?"

"That's the truth, the awful truth."

"I'll find time to teach anyone who wants to learn. It'll take a bit of time to get the school up and running."

"Oh honey, everything takes time." Letty stood up and

walked toward the road. She nodded her head and people came back out of their houses.

"I'll tell the rest but I know they hunger for learning too. Tell Georgie that Letty said it's a fine idea. You best get on home now. It's not that we don't want no white people, we just want no trouble."

"It was nice to meet you and your family, Letty. Good day." Glory shifted Teddy to the other hip. She wasn't used to carrying a child.

She nodded at each person as she walked by, feeling proud of herself for asserting herself instead of being so shy she couldn't talk. Maybe a person could get over being shy. She was almost to the end of the road when Kent rode up.

"What are you doing down here? I've been looking for you." His face grew red as his frown got bigger.

She deflated inside. "I wanted to see if they wanted a teacher."

He jumped down and lifted Glory and Teddy onto the horse. Then he swung up behind them. The feel of his strong arms around her made her feel warm.

"I'm sorry I worried you, Kent."

He kissed the side of her neck and she shivered. "Leave a note or tell someone next time. Did you meet Letty? Nothing goes on without Letty's approval it seems. Did she want you to teach the children?"

"Yes," she answered excitedly. "And she asked if I could teach adults as well. Did you know it was illegal for them to learn to read? That is so wrong. You fought for the south so you must have believed it that they not learn."

"Many of us didn't even own slaves. We were tired of the North thinking they could tell us how to run our states."

"Oh. I guess I need learning myself."

"When we found out you were a teacher, we were all pleased. You are so good with Teddy."

37

"Letty said she's seen Teddy's condition before and to talk to him lots and let him watch what we do and she can tell he's smart."

"Of course he's smart. He takes after me." He chuckled as he reined in the horse. He got down first and then helped Glory down.

For a moment she thought he would not let her go. He gazed into her eyes and grinned. What did he see that made him so happy? She couldn't imagine unless it was Teddy.

KENT TOOK TEDDY FROM HER. "Georgie invited us over for tea or whatever women do. I will only stay for a brief time. It would be good for you and Georgie to get to know one another."

Glory nodded, but she looked uncomfortable.

"Is something wrong? Are you not up for the visit? I could tell Georgie—."

She put her hand on his arm. "I'm fine. I'm not great at small talk and it's always been hard for me to make friends. But my life is here now and I need friends. It's just uncomfortable."

He gave her a warm smile. He thought her shyness to be part of her charm. It had never occurred to him it made her life harder. "Georgie is very nice."

"Yes, I know. I get nervous is all."

He walked up the steps to the Eastman's front porch and Georgie opened the door before he could knock. She had Douglas in her arms and the infant stared at Teddy and smiled.

"Come on in. I'm so glad you came." She took Glory's hand. "I thought we could have Kent move the table in front of the sofa out of the way and we could put the boys on the rug."

"I'm game," Kent agreed before handing Teddy to Glory. He moved the table and was surprised at how much room there was. "Do you think they'll play together?"

Georgie chuckled. "I have no idea." She set Douglas down on the floor and for a moment he looked as though he would cry until he saw Teddy sitting next to him. "Have a seat."

Kent took the large upholstered chair, leaving the sofa for the two women. It would be so nice if Glory had a friend. He watched Glory, and she was practically wringing her hands. "The doc came by."

Georgie's eyes lit up. "Good news I hope."

"We think so," Georgie shared. "Apparently Teddy was left in the crib most of the time. The back of his head is flat. But the doctor thinks he'll catch up just fine. He's too thin so we must work on that too. We're hoping that by watching Douglas, he'll learn a few things."

A wide smile spread across Georgie's face. "I'm so happy for all three of you."

Teddy cried out as Douglas tried to put Teddy's nose in his mouth. Kent gently picked up Douglas and set him back on the floor.

"I hope he doesn't learn everything Douglas does."

They all chuckled and Kent noticed that Glory seemed to have relaxed. New situations were hard. "Well Ladies, I have to get to work. Have a nice visit." He got up and then kissed Glory on the cheek. She delighted him when she blushed. He reached down and ruffled Teddy's hair and left.

"YOU GOT YOURSELF A GOOD MAN. He's equally lucky. Not all

women would have welcomed Teddy. So, tell me what did you think of Joy? Aren't the houses nice?"

"You know I was there already?"

"The grapevine is quick around here. Sondra saw you walking to it. Did you meet Letty?"

"Yes, it was strange at first. No one would talk and they all went into their houses and closed the doors. I knocked but no one answered except for Letty. I take it she's in charge?"

"Yes, she and her husband Darrius. So, tell me more."

"You know Madam Wigg planned for each of us girls to provide an education where ever we ended up. I wondered if there was a need for a teacher so I asked. I was touched by Letty's eagerness for all the children to learn and even the adults. Things are vastly different here than in New York. There was mention you were thinking about building a school?" Glory clutched Georgie's arm. "Look."

Douglas was crawling quickly and Teddy was crawling after him.

"I thought it would take weeks for him to crawl." Her eyes filled with tears. "I'm sorry to be so emotional. I was so worried for him and yesterday it appeared it was one disaster after another."

Georgie put her arms around her. "It's a big change, and you married a man you didn't know. He's a good man. Then you became an instant mother. I think you've earned a good cry."

"I never expected to leave the orphanage. You see, I planned to stay and teach there my whole life. I felt safe there and now I'm feeling lost. I don't even know the rules of polite society. Well, they taught us all that, but I never had to draw from my knowledge to use it in real situations. I'm just plain awkward."

"You'll get the hang of it I promise. Tomorrow Veronica

and I are going berry picking. Would you like to join us? Sondra will watch the children."

Glory sniffled. "I'd like that very much but I must see what Kent thinks."

Teddy crawled to her and lifted his arms up. Glory instantly picked him up and told him how proud she was of him. She stood. "I'll let you know right after breakfast tomorrow if that's fine with you."

"Perfectly fine." Georgie stood and walked them to the door. She opened it and smiled. "I enjoyed our visit."

Glory smiled back. "I did too. I'll see you tomorrow." She walked across the yard feeling buoyant. She actually had a friend. Her emotions ran from relief to happiness.

When she got to the kitchen, she put Teddy down. "I wonder if I cut chicken into tiny pieces if you'll eat it?" Teddy stared at her blankly. "Chicken it is!" She prepared the chicken and cut a small piece of bread. Then she put the plate on the table and picked up Teddy. She hand fed him one small bite at a time and it worked. She stopped for a moment and he pointed to the food. His grandmother must have been a real witch!

Finally, it was naptime and he didn't fuss at all. Glory laid him on the bed with pillows on either side of him and he went fast to sleep. She opened the window to the bedroom so she could hear Teddy if he woke up and then grabbed a basket and went outside.

The woods behind the house would be filled with healing plant. Her heart thumped in anticipation.

She scanned the area. There were many plants she wasn't familiar with in Texas yet. She walked in deeper and smiled when she spotted honey locust. She could make teas from the pods for indigestion and measles and the bark was good for sore throats. She picked pods and with a knife she stripped off some bark. She headed back when she saw palmetto. She gathered some fruit. It was good for inflammation, colds, coughs and headaches. She had a start.

She was almost out of the woods when someone grabbed her from behind. She tried to scream and kick but he covered her mouth with his forceful hand and held her still with the other hand. "Be quiet and I'll let the boy live."

Glory stopped struggling. Fear coursed through her.

"I saw you with the negroes. You don't know your place. You're white and you stick to your own race. You hear me? Things could go very wrong for you and the boy if you go down there again." He pushed her down to the ground and held her face into the dirt. "I'm going now. Don't try to look at me or I'll shoot you dead."

Glory's whole body shook as she lay there. She heard him walk away, and she waited a few minutes to be sure he was out of sight. Hesitantly she stood up and grabbed her basket. She couldn't quite catch her breath. Finally she calmed enough to get back to the house. She was filthy from head to toe.

Quietly she opened the door and walked in.

"Where have you been?" Kent asked a hint of coldness was in his voice.

Before she could answer he strode toward her and his gaze wandered up and down her body. "What the heck happened to you?" He took the basket from her and placed it on the table.

"He warned me to stay out of Joy and stay with white people." Her body trembled. "I was gathering a few plants and such for medicine. He grabbed me from behind and threw me to the ground. It happened within site of the house and he threatened Teddy too. What is going on?"

Kent pulled her to him and held her close, stroking her back. "You're safe now."

"Why would anyone make a threat like that?"

"There's still people down here who don't take kindly to white people helping the freedmen."

"Why?" she whispered, enjoying the feel of his arms around her.

"Near as I can tell, some think they're superior to them."

"Oh, I saw a group of Germans once who were being treated badly. It's not right."

"No it's not. Don't worry; I'll make sure the men know to keep an eye on you and the house. Now look over at the sofa."

She eased out of his strong arms and turned. There were packages all wrapped in brown paper stacked up the whole length of the sofa. Her eyes went wide. "What's all that?"

"You needed new clothes and so did Teddy and I also had Max buy material so you can sew clothes." He took her hand and led her to the packages.

"I've never seen so many before. Kent, you shouldn't have spent your hard earned money on me. I'm not worth fussing over."

He framed her face with his hands and leaned down. He touched his lips against hers. It was a better kiss than she'd gotten yesterday. Then he pressed his lips to hers harder and as a groan come from her, he put his tongue in her mouth. She stilled, not knowing what to do. Finally she copied him and this time he groaned.

IT FELT like a slice of heaven. Kent put his hands in her hair and ended up with a handful of dirt. Slowly he stopped kissing her. "I think a bath might be in order," he teased.

She looked at the dirt and covered her mouth with her hand as her eyes grew wide. "I must look a fright."

"Well, I've seen you looking better," he said with a grin. "I need to find Parker and let him know what happened to you."

She nodded. "I'll get cleaned up so I don't leave dirt on the new things you bought."

"I checked on Teddy he's still sleeping."

"He crawled, and he ate chicken."

He sighed in relief and his heart filled. "That's wonderful news. I'll be right back."

He rubbed the back of his neck as he made his way to the barn. They'd need to search the woods. Glory didn't know how close she came to real harm. They could have taken Teddy too. He couldn't blame her; she didn't know to stay close. Well, actually she was close.

Parker looked up when Kent came into the barn. "What's wrong?"

"Glory wanted to look for herbs for healing or something. She was grabbed and thrown to the ground and told she shouldn't mix with the people in Joy. He threatened Teddy too." His anger bubbled over.

"Where was she?"

"Right behind the house. She had the bedroom window open so she could hear Teddy when he woke. There is a spy on the ranch. You can't even see Joy if you're not on the ranch. We need to do something!"

"Get Max and Willis. We'll make a sweep of the woods. Then we'll need a plan to ferret out the traitor. I'm glad she wasn't hurt. I bet she's upset though. Maybe you should stay with her."

"She's safe. I want to go. Besides, she has all the packages from town to open."

Parker nodded. "Max and Willis should be near the corral. I'll finish up with my horse, Mine, and meet you out front."

Kent quickly found Max and Willis at the corral. They

both stared at him as he approached. He told them what happened.

"Our women need to be safe," Max ground out.

"She went to Joy today? How'd word get to the hooded men so fast?" Willis asked.

"That's a question I want the answer to. Come on, we'll meet Parker at the barn."

They all met at the barn and checked their guns. "I reckon we're ready," Kent said.

"Men spread out and stay low. I doubt he's still there but you never know. We'll need extra guards on duty tonight. I don't like this one bit." Parker said before he led the men into the woods.

They spread out and made their way slowly. Kent found the spot where his wife had been on the ground. He could usually keep his anger in check but he'd love to punch the man in the face. He studied the spot looking for clues. There was a defect or something on the bottom of the man's boots. It showed up in his footprints. The man's feet were larger than Kent's. He stayed low and continued on. He found a few smoked cigarettes on the ground. Had the man been here before or was this his watching place for today?

Kent stood near the cigarettes and turned toward the house. The foliage was thin enough to allow for a good view of the back of his house, Part of the front of Parker's house, the back of the barn and the corral. It might be best to clear the land so there was no place to hide.

Kent showed the other men what he'd discovered. "What should we do?"

Parker shifted from one foot to another as he took in the view the man had. "Your suggestion of clearing the woods is good but we don't have the manpower right now. Willian Cabot reported that most of the freedmen were up to speed on cowboying. We'll need about half of our men to pull guard duty. I'll get Walter Green on making a schedule and taking charge of that. We need eyes everywhere. Someone is spying and we need to get rid of him. If anyone thinks of a good plan, let me know. Kent, does Glory know how to use a rifle?"

"I doubt it. I don't think the school she was at in New York thought it an important subject."

Willis laughed. "It's a funny thing to imagine a school full of women shooting."

"They wouldn't need to shoot in New York City. They won the war, they say," Max commented with a frown.

"Keep vigilant. You know how it goes, no clue is too small." Parker turned to walk back to the compound when he stopped. "Max was anything out of the ordinary in town today?"

"There were less Yankees guarding the entrance to Spring Water. Anson Stack at the general store said he heard they might leave for good. But it was a rumor. Now Nancy Mathers at the dress shop heard they'd be extending their stay. One of their officers keeps asking her out. And Kelly Kingsman at the restaurant wants us to all rise up and shoot the Yankees. So, besides having fewer men at the entrance everything else was the same." Max grinned.

"What happened to you, Max? You've turned into a gossipy old woman," Willis teased. "If this is what marriage is all about you can count me out."

"But you get a house if you marry," Parker told him.

"No house is worth taking a wife. The thought makes me shiver."

Kent's mouth formed a grim line. "You were so competitive when we were seeing who could get a wife the quickest. If I'd known you weren't serious, I wouldn't have bothered. There is value in freedom."

"We might as well head back," Parker instructed.

CHAPTER FIVE

*G*lory took a quick bath, praying the whole time that Kent wouldn't walk in. She got out and realized she had nothing clean to put on. Kent had a couple shirts hanging in the wardrobe so she took the blue one and shrugged it on. Kent was obviously bigger than her. The shirt swallowed her up, he was bigger than she thought. Rolling up the sleeves was an effort, but the shirt covered most of her legs.

Teddy was still napping. He was so angelic in his sleep not that he was bad when he was awake. She had a feeling he'd be a handful when he learned to walk. It wasn't anything she'd never done before. She'd chased down many toddlers at the school.

Next she went to the sofa and stared at the piles of wrapped items. Kent worked hard, and it wasn't right he'd spent so much money on her. Hopefully, most of it was for Teddy. Upon opening the packages she found readymade dresses she held up to her in delight. They were in lovely colors. There weren't as finely crafted as the ones Fae made but they were pretty.

She carefully laid them the over the back of the sofa. Next she found lots of clothes for Teddy and her heart filled. She blushed when she found a few nightgowns for her. They were oh so soft. Her blush deepened when she opened the underclothes. Max had picked it all out. She groaned. How can she ever look at him? He'd know what she had on underneath.

She found the material for clothes and for diapers. There was even a straw hat for her. She wanted to cry when she opened the bar of soap that smelled like flowers. She held it to her nose for a few minutes.

On the bottom she found toys for Teddy. A wooden wagon that had wheels that turned. There was a spinning top and wooden blocks. No one was more generous than her husband. She stared at the pretty material and the sewing items. She knew how to thread a needle. Tonight they'd use up the rest of the food from the wedding and come morning. She shivered.

Would he think her inadequate? All women knew how to cook and sew. She had the chance to learn, but she foolishly read about healing plants.

She put the items away. There was one more package, and it held ribbons for her hair. Her hair was the bane of her existence. No matter how hard she tried, it never appeared tidy. Perhaps the ribbons would help.

She was just finishing hanging her dresses when she heard the door open. She quickly went out to see Kent. When she saw the look of surprise, he wore her face heated.

"I forgot I borrowed you shirt after my bath. I'll go change."

"Glory, come here."

She went to him. "Did you need something?"

"Actually, do you see the latch on the door? I want you to use it when you are in the house alone."

"Yes, Kent. I can do that. Well, I'll be right back."

Before she could turn, Kent took her into his arms and pulled her close. There was so much comfort to be drawn from her husband. His arms were strong and when he pulled her even closer, she could feel that his chest was well muscled.

"Look at me," he whispered.

She raised her gaze to his face. There was a spark in his eyes she wasn't familiar with and before she had time to wonder about it more, he lowered his head until his lips met hers.

His masculine lips were soft. He angled his head and kissed her harder and for a moment she couldn't breathe. He broke off the kiss and stared into her eyes. What did he see? It filled his eyes with some wanting. He captured her lips again and his tongue went into her mouth.

It felt so intimate and she couldn't imagine what a wedding night would be. His kisses made her body hum, and she wanted more kisses which he provided. He hands stroked her back. He stopped kissing and held her tight.

"I'm so glad you weren't hurt in the woods. I was so focused on the man who did this I gave little thought to what I would do if I lost you."

She shivered in his arms. "I'm fine." He sounded like he cared for her and she couldn't think of anything else to say. She laid her cheek on his chest and she heard his heart beating. She should tell him about her flaws. How she couldn't cook or sew and she was clumsy.

Teddy woke up and gave a soft cry.

Kent eased away from her. "I'll get him so you can put clothes on. You're too tempting in my shirt." He turned and went to Teddy.

Stunned, she stayed frozen in place. She was tempting? Either Kent was lying, or he didn't have good vision. She wished she was pretty like Fae, Harriet and Imogene. Was he toying with her? She'd been the object of a few taunts now and again. Maybe he meant it that way? No, Kent wasn't mean.

Kent carried a freshly changed Teddy into the room. He set him on the floor and his eyes opened wide and then filled with joy when Teddy crawled around. "Well, I'll be."

She smiled back at Kent sharing his joy. "I'll go get dressed. Keep an eye on him he's fast." She hurried into the bedroom and she heard Kent chuckle as she closed the door.

She put on her new under items and chose the pink dress to put on. It fit perfectly. Next she brushed her hair and brushed it again, tying it back with a pink ribbon. It wouldn't stay she knew it. Walking in front of the mirror was awkward. She didn't quite look like herself. The color pink seemed to soften all of her sharp angles that made up her face. Her hair was cooperating, imagine that. Perhaps she wasn't as ugly as a toad after all.

She slowly opened the door. What if Kent didn't notice she looked nice? Her thoughts were cut short by Teddy crawling to her as fast as he could and he screeched in delight. Kent was on the floor crawling after Teddy. Kent kept filling her heart. One day they would fill it to the top.

Kent caught Teddy and tickled him. After their laughter died down Kent held Teddy so that they were both watching her. "Doesn't Mama look pretty?" Kent gave her one of his heart-stopping grins.

Tears filled her eyes, but she kept them from falling.

"Glory, what's wrong?"

"No one ever called me pretty and being someone's mama is a huge deal. I wasn't sure what he'd end up calling me. I like mama."

Kent titled his head. "I like being his pa."

"I'll get supper on the table." She hurried away from

Kent's intense stare. He must have something wrong with his eyesight.

There was still fried chicken, biscuits and potatoes. She heated them and then placed them on the table. "It's time to eat." She held her hands out to take Teddy so she could feed him. He was cuddly today. She put him on her lap after she sat at the table.

She feed him small bits of chicken and he was happy to eat it.

"Would you look at that? He's eating chicken. I figured you'd have made porridge for him."

Glory smiled, feeling proud of her accomplishment. "I cut the chicken into the smallest of pieces earlier and he liked it. I bet he'd like most things as long as I make his food into tiny bites."

"I got lucky to have married a woman good with children. Not every woman would have welcomed him as their own. I thank you for that, Glory." Kent's eyes softened.

She glanced away for a moment and then she continued to feed Teddy. "When he likes the food, he can sure eat a lot."

"That's good right?"

She gazed at Kent and found him watching her. "Yes, he needs to gain weight. I'm just sorry for all he's gone through. We'll probably never know what happened."

"We have a pretty good idea. He'll never be neglected again." Kent stood and took Teddy from her. "You need to eat too."

"Thank you," she said without looking up. She didn't know how to act around him. His compliments and his willingness to help with Teddy made her feel uncomfortable. She thought the women did all the child care and men couldn't be bothered. She finished eating and stood to clear away the dishes.

"That's the last of the food that was brought over to us."

Dread washed over her. Breakfast was usually eggs with bacon or sausage and biscuits. Who would make it? She already knew the answer to her own question. She'd have to try and hope for the best.

"You can impress me with your cooking in the morning." He didn't look too hopeful. The coffee she'd made was awful. She couldn't even drink it.

"I made the coffee at the school for many people. I really don't know how much to use for a coffee pot this size."

"Don't fret about it. I can show you in the morning." He sat on the floor again and showed Teddy how to put the blocks on top of another. Teddy liked watching Kent and then would push the blocks so the all fell down. Kent laughed loudly and suddenly stopped. "I can't remember the last time I laughed like that."

She dried her hands and smiled. "Children can bring laughter and joy into one's life."

His eyes wandered from her hair to her shoes. "A good woman can do the same."

Glory crossed the room and sat on the soft sofa. "Are you sure you don't mind that I'll be working at the school?"

He frowned. "Why should I mind? It's a service to the community and I think it'll make you happy."

"This isn't how marriage is supposed to work." She furrowed her brow. "I never thought I'd marry, but I paid attention when it was discussed by the other girls at the school."

His lips twitched. "Oh? How is it supposed to work?"

"The husband is in charge. He makes sure that his family has food on their table and a place to live in. The husband sets the rules and does no work that is women's work. I know a husband can beat a woman and the law can't take him to jail."

Teddy squealed as he knocked the blocks down again.

"I don't beat women so you're safe. I'd be mad if you spent all our money without talking to me. If you'd made arrangements to work without us discussing it, I would have been angry. But like I said, I already knew what you planned to do. I didn't know the details. But just to be safe if you think you need to discuss something with me than you probably should. We'll get better at all this as time goes on. We'll learn to trust each other."

"What about the women's work?" She stared at him trying to remember everything he said.

"I don't mind helping, especially with Teddy. Don't dwell on it. Everything will fall into place for us. None of those girls had been married or lived in a house with married people right?"

She nodded her head.

"Then how do they know what married people do? I don't think in this case they are most reliable source." He cocked his brow.

He was right—

She jumped as she heard breaking glass and dropped to the floor. "What was that?" she whispered.

"Come here and hold on to Teddy while I extinguish the lamps. And see if you two can crawl safely under the table."

She got Teddy to crawl with her and suddenly they were plunged into darkness. He whimpered, and she rocked him while patting his back. She heard Kent moving around and as her eyes got used to the dark, she could see him with a rifle in hand going from window to window.

Her heart thumped painfully against her chest the whole while.

A knock at the door startled her.

"Kent it's me and Willis."

Kent opened the door and pulled them in latching the door behind them.

"What's going on?" Max asked. "We heard the window break."

"Someone threw a rock at the bedroom window. I haven't gone out there looking yet."

"We saw no one," Willis said.

"Let's get Glory and Teddy to Parker's first before we do hunting," Kent said.

Her heart was in her throat as the men escorted her and Teddy to Parker's. She expected someone would shoot them. They quickly went into Parker's house without knocking. Once she shook she couldn't seem to stop. They would think she was a ninny.

"Let's settle you on the sofa," Georgie said gently as she put her arm around Glory's waist.

Glory sat, but she kept her gaze on Kent. It was too dangerous to go into the woods. It became difficult for her to breathe.

Georgie gently took Teddy from her. "Take slower breaths. That's it, nice and slow."

Glory felt better. Kent came and stood in front of her. He leaned down and gave her a deep kiss. "I'll be right back." Before she could say a word, the men were gone. All except Walter Green and he always seemed to be at Georgie's house.

Walter closed the door and locked it. He closed the curtains and put out most of the lamps. He turned the remaining one low. Sondra joined them in the sitting room.

"You've had an eventful day," Walter observed. "Don't worry about Kent, he can handle himself. He's a good man to have with you in a fight."

"A gunfight?" Glory felt the color drain from her face.

"I bet they are long gone," Sondra said.

"I agree," Georgie reassured her. "I would suggest boarding up that window. Or putting bear traps along the back of your house."

"It's my fault. I stirred things up talking about the school. Maybe things should just stay as they are." Glory's voice quavered. She was emotionally exhausted.

"I've found in life nothing ever stays the same," Sondra commented. "The people of Joy are counting on you. How are they supposed to make a better life for themselves if they aren't able to read or do sums? How do they know what they just signed with their X or if they are getting the right pay?"

"She's right," Georgie said. "They are being cheated left and right. It must be hard not knowing who to trust. Besides, I can't wait until they build the school."

"It's all right to be frightened. We all are at one point or another," Sondra added.

"Do you know how to handle a rifle?" Walter asked.

"No I don't."

"Kent probably has that at the top of his list." Walter told her. "Get down!" he shouted as someone kicked in the back door.

Sondra immediately tipped the table on its side. "Glory you and the children stay behind the table."

Glory scrambled as Georgie and Sondra quickly grabbed rifles they had near them. Glory hadn't seen the rifles when she came in. She shook as she sheltered the two boys with her body. There were two rifle shots, and she covered her mouth to keep from screaming. Who was shot? She could hardly breathe.

"Bring him to the front room," Glory shouted. "I'll guard the back door and stay down!"

Staying low Glory peeked around the table. Sondra was practically dragging Walter then she slumped she had him in the front room. Sondra had tears streaming down her face.

"Where was he shot?" Glory asked.

"Out back."

"No, Sondra, where on his body is the bullet?"

"His side. He's losing a lot of blood. I must get the bullet out," Sondra's voice trembled.

"Do you know how?"

"Of course not," Sondra snapped at Glory.

"I do. Sondra come and switch places with me and I'll tend to Walter."

Sondra shook her head.

"Do it now!" Glory exploded. "Take the rifle with you just in case."

Sondra did as Glory wanted and went back behind the table. She spoke quietly to the two little ones.

Glory immediately ripped Walter's shirt. Then she took two diapers and pressed down hard on his wound. She waited a few minutes the raised the cloths to see how bad off he was. The bullet had gone in and then out the back. She grabbed more cloths and put pressure on both bullet holes. At least he wouldn't have to suffer from her digging out the bullet.

Walter groaned. "I need to protect you women."

"Not now, Walter. You need to stay still until we can turn on the lights," Glory gently told him.

"But—"

"Walter, stay put! Don't make me come out there and hit your head until you understand!" Sondra shouted.

Glory smiled. Walter seemed stunned, but he relaxed his shoulders

"Georgie, how's it going?" Walter yelled.

"I don't think they are out there anymore. I'm not going get too close to the broken door to check."

"Good plan," Walter called. The pain was now clear in his voice.

The blood was clotting and Glory hoped there was whiskey in the house to clean the injury and for the pain of stitches. At first light, she'd get alder bark and make a poultice for the wound. Funny how she could stitch a person up but couldn't sew cloth.

A knock on the front door followed by Parker asking to be let in startled Glory and she jumped before she rose and opened the door. Parker stared at her. "Where are my wife and child?" His eyes narrowed.

"Georgie is guarding the back door and Douglas is behind the table with Sondra." Glory told him. He didn't acknowledge her but instead he raced to the back.

Kent came in looking tired. There were circles under his eyes. Maybe they were from worry. He hugged Glory to him but as soon as he saw Walter; he went to his side.

"Sondra is there any whiskey in the house? I'll need a needle and thread." Glory knelt next to Kent.

"Is he going to be all right?" Kent asked.

"Yes. I will stitch him up and then tomorrow we need to get the bark and leaves of an Alder tree."

Sondra handed her the whiskey and shook her head. "I've never heard of using anything like that. No, I think fresh air is the best thing."

"I studied botany and herbs. I healed many at the orphanage. I know what I'm doing. Put Walter's head in your lap so he can drink whiskey. Not all of it mind you. I still need to clean the wound."

Sondra gave her a look of doubt as she put the bottle to Walter's lips. He took a deep swig and then sputtered. He took another swig and another.

"No, there will not be any witch medicine used on my Walter. We don't even know you. It's possible you led those men here tonight. I can't say for sure I trust you. There's something shifty about you." Sondra glared at her.

Sondra's words hurt and Glory half expected Kent to speak up for her but he remained silent. Even after she gazed at him, he turned his gaze so he wasn't looking at her.

Sondra threaded the needle and after elbowing Glory away she started to stitch up Walter.

Glory wanted to tell her she needed to wash the wound with the whiskey but she could tell by the set of Sondra's jaw she wouldn't welcome her advice.

Glory got up and picked up a sleeping Teddy. She held him close. "I'm going home," she whispered to Kent.

He looked up at her his brow furrowed. "Now?"

Her throat felt raw, and she didn't have much time before a sob would follow. She didn't answer; she walked out the door. She was halfway to her house when Kent grabbed her elbow.

"You don't just take my son like that! Give him." The fury on his face frightened her.

She handed Kent his son and kept walking to the house. As soon as she had, the door closed the tears fell. It had all been too much and Sondra wounded her beyond measure. Kent also had a hand in it. Her shoulders slumped as she dragged her feet to the bedroom.

It pained her to see the blood on her pink dress but it was just a dress. After putting her nightgown on she grabbed quilts and went into the other bedroom. She made sure the door was closed and made herself a pallet. She lay down, covered herself with one quilt and sobbed.

In what way was there something shifty about her? What did Sondra mean? Didn't Sondra just see her pressing on Walter's wounds with all her might to get the bleeding to stop? Yet she couldn't be trusted. As wounding or maybe more so, Kent had turned from her. He was ashamed of her. He lied when he called her a good women and pretty. All his kisses were lies too. He was the one who couldn't be trusted, and she was married to the man until death.

Her heart hurt and her soul ached and her sobs grew louder. She'd opened her heart to everyone too easily. It was like the most painful slap across the face when he said that. She couldn't stay yet she couldn't leave. Somehow she needed to protect her heart from everyone before they tore it out of her.

She heard Kent come home with *his* son and she quieted down and waited but Kent never came into the room. She was the stupidest woman alive, hoping he'd come in to talk to her, to hold her, to apologize to her. Her whole body hurt. She would find an Alder tree come first light. Kent would have to make breakfast for him and his son.

Walter was bound to get an infection and the only way she knew to heal him was turning the bark into a poultice. They wouldn't allow her to use it but she'd feel better knowing she had some on hand just in case.

It would be awkward going to see Walter with Sondra there. She wouldn't go. She wished the school was built. She needed to keep busy, so she didn't feel her shattered heart. She was such a fool. Kent kissed her and made her feel things. Swallowing hard, she turned over. He'd probably want a wedding night, and she wasn't sure how she could allow him to ever touch her again.

CHAPTER SIX

*K*ent woke up finding Teddy staring and smiling at him. Loving a child was easy. Glory had to see that Sondra had a point, they didn't really know her. He got up and changed Teddy and got them both dressed. Glory was intelligent she probably figured it was words of fear and she should just forget it.

He'd promised to show Glory how to make coffee. "Come on, Teddy lets go see Mama." He walked out of the bedroom and Glory wasn't there. The bedroom door was open, but she wasn't there. "Now where do you think Mama went? To the outhouse?"

He waited a minute and made the coffee. He could show her another time. Teddy looked hungry to Kent made him some porridge. By the time Teddy was done eating, Glory still hadn't returned.

"I guess we need to go check on her. Maybe she went to see how Walter's doing."

Teddy smiled at him and babbled. Kent felt the joy of Teddy's progress down to his toes. Kent couldn't wait to see the smile on Glory's face.

They checked the outhouse and then went to Parker's house. Veronica answered the door and let him in.

"Everyone but Max and I are asleep. It was a long night for them all," she told him. She smiled as she touched Teddy's cheek.

"Glory isn't here?"

Veronica paled. "I wouldn't expect her to be. She talked about being like a doctor and wanting to put something that could be poison on Walter. I wasn't here, but that's the story I got."

His heart dropped. "Well, take care and I'll be around if needed."

"See you later Kent, you too Teddy." Veronica waved before she closed the door.

"I hope your mama didn't leave the ranch. I know she was crying but women do that. Tell you what; let's go look at the horses while we wait for Mama."

The horses thrilled Teddy. He petted them, grabbed their manes and tried to bite them. Kent laughed while teaching him the right way. The whole time Kent was worried about Glory. It was too dangerous for her to be alone out there.

Once again he knocked on Parker's door. This time Georgie answered it. Kent explained that he needed to look for Glory and Georgie's face became stricken.

"Here give me Teddy. Anything could happen to her out there. Tell her not to worry. If I had thought of it, I would have found an alder tree too. I heard what went on and my heart goes out to her. She helped and then no one wanted to trust her." She stared at Kent. "You should have stood up for her. You're all she has. Go find her and make up with her. Then ask her if she would bring her healing herbs. Walter has an awful fever and his wounds look too red for my liking."

"What about the doctor?" Kent asked as he shifted from one foot to the other.

"He's busy delivering a baby. The first baby and those always take a long time. You tell her she has a friend in me and the rest feel bad about what happened."

Kent's shoulders slumped. "I will. See you." He walked down the steps feeling like a young boy who had just been chastised. Georgie was right; he should have told Sondra to stop talking. He should have said no one is as trustworthy as his wife. There was a lack of good doctors in the south and healers were always a welcome sight.

What type of plant was she looking for? No, it wasn't a plant it was a tree. He ran his fingers through his hair as he tried to remember what she said. Alder tree? He didn't know one tree from another. He doubted she went into the woods behind their house again. There were more woods on the other side of Joy. Taking a deep breath, he headed for Joy.

He nodded at the women and children as he went by. He was near the end of the houses when Letty's daughter, Hannah stopped him.

"Mr. Sandler!" She ran to him. "My mama said to tell you they went into the woods right where the fence post for the pasture is. My ma has the leaves but not the bark for Mr. Green. Mrs. Sandler looked so sad. She's not going to leave is she? I want to go to school and get some learnin'."

"She's not going anywhere. Thank you for telling me where they went. I'm sure I can have your mom back to you soon." He smiled and nodded to the little girl before he walked to the pasture and found the fence post. He'd never noticed the well-worn path into the woods before.

He walked down the path for a while before he heard laughter. It felt wonderful to hear Glory's laugh. He had a lot of apologizing to do. He should have made sure she was fine last night. He really hadn't known what to say to her so he took the easy way out.

"Morning ladies. You're right where Hannah said you'd be."

"It's about time you came to find your wife," Letty admonished.

Kent only had eyes for Glory. He swallowed hard at the hurt on her face. Her eyes were puffy, and she seemed miserable.

"Well, now we got what we need, I'm going home and let you two talk." Letty picked up her basket and headed down the path.

Glory studied her basket as if there was a prize in it. He waited, but she didn't look up. He wasn't any good with women.

"I'm glad you didn't get into any trouble this time in the woods."

She glanced up with narrowed eyes and lips that formed a grim line.

"You left really early this morning. I was going to show you how to make coffee, remember?"

This time she didn't acknowledge him. He was too awkward in these situations.

"Georgie says hello."

She lifted her head and stared at him as though she was waiting for him to say something more. His face heated. What else could he say?

"Georgie told me to make up with you and then have you bring the plants. She said it really works." He smiled confident she'd be happy.

Glory scowled at him and walked right by him, pulling her skirt so it didn't touch him. She marched down the path.

"Glory, did you want to wait for me? I could escort you!" She didn't stop or give any indication she heard him. He needed to ask Max or Parker about this husband thing. Yes, he was missing something and he couldn't figure out what to do.

GLORY HURRIED HOME and prepared the poultice for Walter. Kent didn't mention how Walter was fairing but if Georgie asked her to bring *her plants*, He probably wasn't doing as well as he could be. She put it all in a jar and started for the Eastman house. Kent never said a word about her sleeping in the other room. All he cared about was his coffee. She'd have to distance herself from Teddy and it would tear her heart. In the long run it would protect her from more heartache.

Georgie answered the door. "I put water on to boil. I have willow bark to make into a tea for his pain."

"Oh, good that will help. I made the poultice. Let me look at his wounds."

Glory followed Georgie into the spare bedroom. Sondra was sitting in a chair next to the bed and she glared at Glory. Glory didn't have time for Sondra's drama.

She went to the other side of the bed, pulled back the blanket and the sheet that were covering Walter. He was bare-chested and it probably should have bothered her but it wasn't his chest she wanted to see.

Slowly and carefully she removed the bandages. Infection was setting in. She put a hand to his forehead, and he was hot.

"Cold water and clean cloths?" Georgie inquired.

"Yes, and fresh bandages to lie over the poultice." Georgie nodded and left the room.

Sondra continued to glare at her. "This is your fault. Whatever you did last night made him worse. Even your husband thought so."

Glory glanced up and her gaze met Kent's. He stood leaning against the door frame. He pushed off from the frame and walked to Glory's side.

"I never said that, Sondra. In fact, I should have told you to have confidence in my wife. She healed many at the orphanage."

Sondra shook her head. "Children sniveling with colds differ greatly from a man with a gunshot wound,"

Kent took the water and cloths from Georgie. "I'll get the bandages and the tea." She hurried from the room.

Glory took the basin of water from him and set it on the small table next to the bed. She then took the cloths from him. After wetting the cloth she bathed Walter's face, neck and shoulders.

"In fact, I have dealt with a few gunshot wounds before. A couple orphans who were living on the street took apples from a store and the owner got them both with buckshot. It wasn't pretty."

"I don't want to make assumptions here but I bet no one wants me to bathe his chest so one of you two will have to do it. Avoid his wound. I will keep cooling his head."

"I should do it. You two aren't married Sondra," Kent said.

"He likes me better," she retorted.

Glory wet two cloths and handed each of them one. "I don't care who does it. It's vital we cool him down." She was surprised at her urge to slap Sondra. She'd never hit a woman in her life. Glory couldn't even look at them; she continued to concentrate on Walter's head. She placed the cloth over his forehead, allowing it to cover some of his hair too.

Georgie came back with the willow bark tea as Walter woke up. "What's going on?" He demanded. He looked as mean as a bear.

Sondra took his hand. "they shot you last night. I've been trying to get you well ever since."

Walter's brow furrowed. He glanced around the room. "I thought Glory was going to patch me up."

Sondra leaned forward and whispered. "She must have done something wrong. You have a fever and an infection."

Glory pretended she didn't hear, it hurt her but her feelings. "I'll take that tea, Georgie. Now he's awake, it'll be easy to get him to drink it."

Walter stared at Glory and he narrowed his eyes. "You wanted to poison me. I was in and out last night but I remember that part."

Her stomach rebelled, and she had to swallow hard. She handed the cup back to Georgie and hurried from the room. She didn't stop until she was back home and in the spare bedroom. She needed Fae, Imogene and Harriet more than ever. They'd sheltered her from anyone who tried to be mean to her. Now she didn't know how to react. She did not understand what to do.

She didn't even know where Teddy was. Madam Wigg would be so disappointed in her. Glory sighed. She couldn't hide in the bedroom all day. She picked up her pink dress and put it in a metal tub in the kitchen and then filled the tub with cold water. There wasn't much hope that the blood would come out but she needed to try.

Next she made bread. She could that and while it was baking, she'd figure out how to make clothes for Teddy. She wasn't doing it for Kent's sake. It was for Teddy's sake. She put an apron on and made the dough. It would have to rise and then she'd punch it down and bake it.

She'd hoped by keeping busy she wouldn't have to think about everything. She shouldn't have talked to Letty and she shouldn't have gone into the woods. There was so much in the South she didn't understand. She'd just have to be her own friend.

She wrote to the orphanage and see about getting school supplies sent down. They didn't need a building. She could teach them anywhere. Too bad they stole her bag. She'd had a reading primer in it.

Finally, the bread was ready to go into the oven. After that was taken care of she sorted through all the material and found cloth for Teddy's frocks and material to make more diapers. Using one of Teddy's dresses she measured a pattern bigger and shorter. After all, he'd be walking soon enough. It was much easier to make baby and toddler clothes than pants and a shirt when he got older.

She was good at the pattern and pinning together part. It was the sewing itself that gave her fits. She set aside the pieces and cut the cloth for diapers instead. These needed to be hemmed and maybe she could practice making straight seams.

She took the bread out and let it sit. The whole house smelled of fresh bread. Then she glanced at her pink dress. It didn't look as though much of Walter's blood had soaked off. It was strange that neither Kent nor *his* son had come home. Had Teddy been fed?

Guilt filled her momentarily before anger took its place. She wasn't the one who insulted or ignored others. She was the one who tried to help. A tear trailed down her face, and she wiped it away in frustration. She'd act as though she was just a caretaker or servant. She didn't want to be Kent's wife and Kent didn't want her to be Teddy's mother.

She'd do what she must until the school started. That was something she could control. She could start with reading to the students; someone was bound to have a book around. She could teach them the names of different plants and tell them which ones could help to heal. They could repeat the alphabet after her and learn to count without slates or desks.

Tomorrow she'd talk to Letty and see when the best time to start would be. It felt better having a plan. She picked another diaper up and sewed the hem.

KENT WAS RIDING a quarter horse named Shade back to the barn. He'd been out checking fences and thinking. Georgie had taken over when Glory ran out on Walter. The poultice was applied, and she was bandaged again. Walter even drank the tea. Georgie had high hopes the fever would break.

He'd felt a hint of coolness from Georgie. She wasn't happy with him but Sondra and Walter thanked him over and over for helping. It didn't all sit well with him. He did nothing. Sondra was usually so kind and caring but she'd done an about face after Walter was hurt. Sondra was probably frightened, but she'd treated Glory poorly.

He wasn't sure what to do about Glory. He had no business being married. He didn't know a thing about it. His parents were almost never in the same room and they hardly talked to each other. He didn't want that for himself or Glory but he didn't know how to fix it.

When he got to the barn, a cowboy named Crumb offered to take care of Shade. Kent was grateful. Crumb was a good man.

Kent hurried to Veronica and Max's house. The door opened before he knocked and Veronica had Teddy all ready to go.

"Did something happen?" Kent asked.

"No, it's just that I couldn't get anything done. Bridey and Teddy are both very fast and the never went in the same direction. They both refused to nap. They wore me out." She smiled. "I hope Glory is feeling better."

Kent snuggled Teddy to him. "We need to go see Mama. I don't know what to say to her."

Teddy nodded. "Mama."

Kent smiled widely. "That's right. We will see Mama." He walked faster. Glory would love hearing Teddy call her mama.

The door was locked, so he knocked. He heard it being unlatched, but the door didn't open. Frowning, he opened the door and there sat Glory sewing. She didn't look up when they entered the house.

There was material all over the table and the floor. "Looks like you've been busy."

She glanced up at him. "Yes." She said and went back to sewing.

He grew irritated and put Teddy down on the floor. "Is supper ready?"

"I made bread. Help yourself."

He went to the counter by the stove and there was a loaf of bread there. "I meant where is the meal you made for us to eat?" His voice grew louder.

Glory picked up the scraps of material and set it all in one pile while she set other sewing in another. Teddy crawled toward her and she smiled at him but turned and walked in the other direction.

What was she doing? "Didn't you make anything for Teddy to eat?" He was at his wits end.

She picked up all the piles. "He's your son. You said so last night." She went into the spare room and closed the door.

Kent felt crushed. He wanted to talk to her and work it out but she'd already decided about him and Teddy. So that was it? He never should have gotten married. Winning a bet and getting a house wasn't worth it. He watched Teddy play with his blocks. Kent was glad he had the house for Teddy's sake.

"Well, I can make porridge for us." He might as well have been talking to the air. No one seemed to care.

He got busy cooking and reined in his temper for Teddy's sake. He didn't want his son scared. What did Glory mean by saying Teddy was his son? Didn't she want to be his mother anymore? His heart cracked as he gazed upon his son. Teddy had had enough bad things in his life already. He didn't deserve Glory's irrational anger. He didn't deserve it one bit.

After Teddy went to sleep Kent planned to have a chat with his so-called wife.

CHAPTER SEVEN

Glory sat on her pallet for a long while but when Teddy cried and she flew out of the room to comfort him. He was just an innocent child. She sat down on the floor next to him and lifted him into her arms and held him to her.

"Mama." Teddy hiccupped.

Did she hear him correctly? Did he call her mama? She turned toward Kent and he nodded.

"I love you, Teddy and I'm sorry I was out of sorts when you came home." She kissed his cheek and rubbed his back. Her heart expanded even more as she held him to her. Her resolve to just be a servant vanished.

"He's only been here a few days. I'm surprised he called me Mama."

Kent gave her a slight smile. "He can feel how much you love him. It's a nice feeling until it ends." His smile soured.

She closed her eyes, took a deep breath, let it out slowly and gazed at him. It would be so easy to say nothing and hope for the best but even as shy as she could be she fought for what she wanted. He had to know how she felt or nothing would ever be fixed.

"Kent, you broke my heart. I didn't take my feelings away, they were pushed away. I've always been a trusted, wanted, friend. I never should have come here. If I hadn't, none of what befell Walter would have happened. I know I'm the one at fault for all the trouble but to make me feel like an unwanted stranger and calling this child yours. The hurt still pierces me. I guess it hurts so much because I thought we would be a family. I should have realized you never invited me to be Teddy's mother. I'm not totally convinced you ever wanted a wife." She had no words left. Tears trailed down her face and Teddy traced them with his little finger.

She watched as Kent quietly left.

"Teddy, when I was a little girl I wished and wished for a family. I had my heart set on a mother and father. I'd also hoped for a brother or sister. Then as I grew older, I grew shyer, and I didn't want to leave the orphanage. I eventually became a teacher there."

Teddy smiled and waved his hands around. "Mama."

Glory kissed him. "You honor me, Teddy. I never imagined I'd be a mother. I am your mother and I'll always be your mother. Callous words can't change the bond we are building. I love you, little one."

She stood up with Teddy in her arms and locked the door like Kent had told her. It was dark outside. The window in their bedroom had been boarded over and reinforced. Kent had also insisted on closing the curtains when it was dark outside. As she closed them a chill rampaged through her body. She had a bad feeling, and it wasn't just about her relationship with Kent.

She went into the bedroom and changed Teddy into a sleeping gown. Then she placed the two pillows on the bed and put him in the center. Turning the lamp low she sat and sang to him. He fell right to sleep.

Her shoulders slumped after she left the bedroom. It was too quiet in the house. She loved the fresh wood scent. Normally she'd be laughing and talking with Harriet, Fae and Imogene. She said a silent prayer for their happiness. Finally she grabbed more diapers that needed hemming. She still had to admit to Kent that she couldn't cook.

Maybe she was a fraud. She couldn't sew correctly or make a meal. Kent most likely assumed she did both. She knew she would be a good teacher, and she'd talk to Kent about starting school soon. They needed to work together and trying to understand each other. Otherwise her life would be as silent and empty as she felt at the moment.

There was a loud thud against the back of the house. Fear filled her as she checked on Teddy. He slept peacefully.

Someone was outside, and she wasn't sure if there were guns in the house. Even if she had one unless someone loaded it she wouldn't be able to shoot it and she wouldn't hit anything she aimed at. She grabbed a sharp cooking knife and put it in her apron pocket. It didn't make her feel any safer.

Where was Kent? Was he checking on Walter and listening to Sondra's reason for not liking her? That could probably take a while even though Sondra hardly knew her. Glory thought to make friends here, but it didn't look that way.

There was another thump on the side of the house. She grabbed her knife and walked toward the window. The next thing she knew she went flying to the floor. Stunned for a moment she didn't realize the extent of her injury. The pain in her shoulder excruciating and she knew she'd stabbed herself but she was afraid to look to see how bad it was.

Slowly she sat up and pulled the knife out of the front of her. Blood gushed, and she felt faint. She could doctor others but her own blood made her woozy. The knife clattered to the floor. She walked on her knees to a chair and used it to left herself up. Another dress with blood on it.

Did they have any whiskey? She didn't even know where to look. It was hard to unbutton her dress with one hand but she did it. Then she took off her chemise. She stood up and grabbed a few unhemmed diapers and her needle and thread. It would not go well without something to lessen her pain.

While applying pressure to her knife wound she put water on to boil. It exhausted her. Next she put the palmetto fruits she'd picked and put them in a jar. She poured boiling water on them and shook her head. It would take hours before she could use it. She needed comfrey leaves. She should have gathered the leaves when she saw them.

She could hardly stand but she managed to put a knife, a needle and thread into the water. Feeling lightheaded she sat down on a wooden chair and changed out the cloth. Maybe she should pick a few of the leaves. The plant was by the back corner of the house.

It would be stupid to go outside just about as stupid as stabbing yourself. Her shoulder and arm were throbbing, and it took everything she had not to cry. After she fished the items out of the water and put them on a clean towel on the table. At least she staunched the bleeding enough for her to stitch it.

Her stomach churned, but it had to be done. She got up one more time and found a piece of wood she could bite down on to keep from screaming. With the needle threaded she put it through her skin. *Oh no, how will I do this?* One stitch meant going through two places with the needle.

It would have been better if she could have done it

quickly but the angle made it too hard. She'd probably have to be stitched again by someone who could see the cut better. After every stitch she took a deep breath and let it out. At one point she mopped her forehead with a clean cloth. Thank goodness Teddy had slept through it. Finally she was able to tie it off. It even hurt to cut the thread.

Just a little more time and she'd be done. Her hands shook as she bandaged herself. All she wanted was to lie down, but she'd have to unlock the door for Kent. She could at least put her chemise back on. As hard as she tried she couldn't get her arm through it. The pain was bad but not as bad as when she was stitching it. Finally she took the piece of wood out of her mouth.

IF ONLY HE could ride to town and drink at the saloon. Maybe he'd feel better. Kent's chest hurt when he thought about Glory's pain. He never meant to hurt her, never, and he had to make it right. He'd spent the last two hours brushing down the horses and thinking. He'd have to ask for her forgiveness. Part of him rejected the idea. He wasn't good at saying he was sorry but another part knew he had to so they could grow toward each other.

He sighed heavily as he rubbed the back of his neck. He'd best get it over with. He walked the distance from the barn to the house at a slower pace than usual. He knocked on the door and for a minute he was certain she would not let him in.

The door opened, and he'd seen no one so pale. His jaw dropped, and he scooped her up into his arms and put her on the sofa.

"What happened? Were you attacked? I told you to keep

the door locked. Where's Teddy?" He didn't wait for an answer he checked on Teddy and was relieved he was sleeping. He came back and sat on the table in front of the sofa.

He took her chemise from her and saw the ugly stitches right under her shoulder bone. He looked lower and saw her lovely breasts. But now wasn't the time. "How did this happen and who stitched you up?"

"It was me. There was a loud thud against the bedroom wall and it scared me so I put a sharp knife in my pocket. Then the thud was at the side of the house. I took out the knife and was going to peek out the window when I tripped and fell. I stabbed myself."

Kent pushed the hair back from her forehead. There was so much pain in her eyes. "Who stitched you?"

Her breathing was shaky. "I did it. There was no one else." Tears leaked out and ran down her face.

"It looks deep. It must have been hard to stitch yourself. There are big gaps between the stitches."

She nodded and groaned. "I thought might be the case. I had nothing for the pain and no way to clean it. There is a comfrey bush out back and if I could only get some leaves, it'll help with the healing."

Kent stroked her wet cheek with the back of his hand. "I've got whiskey." He went to the cupboard and reached high and deep. "I guess you couldn't find it."

"I don't know if I could keep it down at this point. My stomach wants to empty itself."

He grabbed some paper that had been wrapped around the items from the store. Then he found his pencil. "Here, draw the leaves for me."

"I'm so sorry, Kent. I'm clumsy. I've always been this way." Her voice was sorrowful.

"It's not your fault. I should have been here. It was an unfortunate incident."

She nodded slowly and drew a picture of the leaves.

"Should I get Georgie? What about the bark tea?"

"I want no one to know. It'll just be something else for them to talk about."

He was trying to be patient, but he wasn't sure how much longer he'd be able to keep calm. "They are our friends. I know it's been a rough couple of days and things were said but no one meant them, including me." He kissed her cheek and took the drawing. After lighting a lamp he opened the front door. "Leave it unlocked. I don't want you to move."

He sprinted across the way to Parker's house and knocked on the door. Sondra opened it and let him in without a word.

Parker jumped up from his chair. "What happened?"

"I need Georgie and her bark tea. My wife fell and stabbed herself. I also need her to show me which leaves are comfrey leaves. I know where the shrub is supposed to be but Glory was shaking so badly I can't tell a thing from her drawing."

Parker poured him some whiskey as Georgie gathered the tea. Kent downed it all in one swig and followed Georgie out the door.

"Parker, come by after a while so you can walk me home," Georgie said as Parker held the door watching them leave.

"I'll be there."

"Now, Kent where is the bush?"

"Here, follow me. It's at the back corner of the house." It surprised him to find it right where Glory said it was. And it was growing with nothing near it.

Georgie quickly stripped off a big handful of the leaves. "She must be in pain." She hurried to the front door.

Kent took long strides to keep up with Georgie and was right behind her when she went inside.

She handed him a jar with willow tree bark. "Steep this in some hot water while I check her out."

Kent did it right away.

"You poor dear," Georgie was saying when he joined them.

"Kent it looks deep. It's a good thing we got the comfrey otherwise she probably wouldn't heal properly. We need to take the stitches back out. Glory why didn't you wait for Kent to come back?"

Tears filled Glory's eyes again. "We had words, and I didn't know if he'd be back."

Her words jolted through him. "I'd be back. I'm sorry if you thought that."

She gave him a wavering smile. "I don't know what to think anymore."

"Kent, can you help me with the tea?" Georgie asked.

He followed her until she stopped at the table. "Look at all that blood. She will be weak for some time. How she could take care of herself is beyond me. Most people would have had to lie down, unable to find the strength. She's quite a woman. Now go back and hold her hand while I get the tea ready then I'll make a paste out of the leaves. I'll need those stitches out too but we'll wait until the tea takes effect and helps with the pain."

He nodded and picked up a pair of scissors from the side table where Glory had her sewing.

"Let's do this in the kitchen. I don't want blood on the sofa." Glory suggested. She sounded exhausted.

"Darlin' I think you might be right." He put the scissors in his pocket and gently lifted her. She laid her head on his chest and he hugged her tighter to his body. He could have lost her. Life in Texas could be dangerous. He needed to be more grateful for what he had. Georgie was right; Glory was a very strong woman.

He set her down on a chair and gently kissed her cheek. "It's not fair you have to go through the pain again."

She weakly smiled at him. "I'll have something to help with the pain. Why hide the whiskey? Did you think me to be a drinker?"

"I know this sounds stupid now, but I wanted it out of Teddy's reach." He put up his hand. "I know before you say anything he isn't even walking and it would be years before he could reach for anything on the lowest shelf. I guess I didn't think we'll have much use for it."

"I should have gathered more leaves and roots and had some of them steeping. I wasn't prepared for an emergency and I should have been." Glory leaned back against the chair.

Georgie placed a steaming mug in front of Glory. "You sip on this while I make the comfrey into a paste. I'm glad you knew where to find it. It's very dark outside."

Kent felt better knowing Glory was in good hands.

GLORY TOOK small sips of the willow bark tea. She felt its soothing effect take place. As she finished the beverage, Georgie was busy grinding up the leaves using a wooden bowl and the handle from a large wooden spoon. She added a splash of water to it and made a healing paste.

"Are you ready?" Georgie picked up the scissors and cut the stitches. As soon as she picked all the thread off she turned to Kent. "I'll need that whiskey now."

Kent handed it to her, and she poured some onto the gash. Glory reached out her hand trying to find something to hold on to. Finally she found Kent's hand. Taking hold she squeezed it as the pain traveled through her.

"You've quite the grip," Kent said through gritted teeth.

"How did you not scream when you did it without a pain reliever?"

"I bit on a piece of wood you had in a pile for whittling." She gripped his hand again. "It's not as bad this time." She stared into his eyes as she winced. He cared. She could tell that he cared.

"I have good news for you, Glory," Georgie said as she stitched. "We will have the school built!"

"That is good news," Glory said through gritted teeth.

"It will be just like a barn raising. Everyone will help and we'll feed them. Did that hurt? I'm almost done. It'll be next Saturday. I'm so excited. Education will make such a difference to the people of Joy."

"I heard there was another teacher. What happened?" Glory asked as she squeezed Kent's hand.

"I hate to speak badly about someone but he wasn't up to teaching. He explained he expected them to all sit down and pay attention or he'd paddle them or hit them with a ruler. Those poor children have been through enough violence in their lives. You're not the ruler type are you?"

Glory shook her head. Perspiration was forming on her forehead. Kent noticed and gently dabbed at it with a cloth.

"The freedmen have so many hopes and dreams wrapped up in that school. I know it'll be a success. Glory, you seem to be a nurturing type of woman and that's what they need." Georgie put the comfrey paste on the stitched cut.

"Did the other teacher plan to teach adults as well?" Glory asked as she relaxed.

"No, he didn't think it proper to teach adults. He was a certified teacher."

"Hogwash!" Both Kent and Georgie stared at her with wide eyes. "I'm a certified teacher and I feel it's my duty to teach anyone that wants to learn. All the teachers From the Wigg Academy were taught to think the same. I need to send a letter to Madam Wigg and let her know we are building the school and we need supplies. I did not understand that they only printed school books in the North. I need slates for the children but I thought maybe until we get all the supplies I could teach them outside, learning about botany and reciting the alphabet and getting familiar with numbers."

Georgie bent and kissed Glory's cheek. "What a wonderful idea!"

Glory felt prideful. Everything would work out. She glanced at Kent, her marriage too.

"I'm going home. Kent make her more tea before she goes to bed then more in the morning. I'll stop by and put more paste on. Glory you take it easy. Don't you dare pull those stitches by trying to do any work. In fact, Kent you'll probably want to put her arm in a sling." Georgie gathered her things.

"Wait, I'll walk you home." Kent kissed Glory's cheek, grabbed his hat and left with Georgie.

Glory smiled. The school would be built soon and then she'd be too busy to worry about Kent. They won't have time for each other and that just might be a good thing. She was deciding where she'd sleep when Kent came back home.

"I'll get your nightgown and help you into it. Then I'll tuck you in with Teddy. I can either sleep in the bed or on the floor where you've been sleeping. It's your choice."

He had a look of hope in his eyes and she did the right thing. "You can sleep in the bed with us. It's where you belong."

Kent knelt before her and cupped her face in his big hands. He smiled at her and she felt the smile all the way to her toes. Leaning in he kissed her. It was a long, deep soul searing kiss. As he pulled away, he stared into her eyes.

"Glory I'm so sorry for things I said and did. You and Teddy come first and I won't lose sight of that again. I know you're shy and uncomfortable and yet you helped Walter and you never got any thanks. I'm thanking you for helping my friend. It was a generous thing to do and I'm learning that's your way- being generous." He chuckled. "You look half asleep. Let me get your gown and carry you to bed.

CHAPTER EIGHT

wo days later Glory stood under a big willow tree smiling at her students. There were more children than she'd imagined. Most looked eager to be there, but it was disconcerting to have armed men guarding them. The children were repeating the alphabet after her. Glory's heart filled. Madam Wigg was right to send her out to teach.

She only taught for a few hours in the morning. She needed to find someone to watch Teddy, and she wanted to allow the students to get a taste of what school was.

"You all did wonderful today and you make me proud. I will see you tomorrow." She saw a mother with tears in her eyes and quickly made her way to her.

"Hello Mrs. Harkins. Did I say or do anything to bring you distress?" Glory asked gently.

"No. It's just no one ever said they were proud of my boys before. In fact, it was threatened that they'd be sold off and taken from me. I have two other boys I ain't seen in over four years now. My James would be about five and my Manor about four. But I thank you for what you said. Call me Lucy."

"Lucy I can't begin to understand what your family has

been through since I lived in New York. I can ask around about two boys named Harkins. `

"That's mighty kind of you. But I don't think they'd be named Harkins. Most likely they'd be Roebucks now."

Glory furrowed her brow. "Were they adopted? I don't understand."

"They were sold to Mr. Roebuck. Some have changed their names and haven't kept the last name of their owners but others who are hoping to find family keep the name to help in the search. Maybe my boys hear the Harkins are here and they come back."

Glory gave Lucy's hand a quick squeeze. "I'll keep your boys in my prayers and pass their names along to my husband. He might know or he might hear of them."

"Thank you, Mrs."

"Oh, call me Glory. It was nice to meet you, Lucy, but I have a little boy at home that needs tending to. I'll see you tomorrow."

"Yes, tomorrow, Miss Glory." Lucy smiled.

Walking back to the house Glory couldn't understand how Lucy could smile. Glory had heard of such practices but she'd never known someone it happened to. Those boys had to have been babies when they were taken from her.

Glory's heart hurt for that family. How exactly did slavery work? The owners were allowed to sell their children? She couldn't imagine what it must have been like.

Her eyes widened as her heart filled with joy. "Well, look at you, Teddy!" Kent was holding both of Teddy's hands while Teddy walked. It was a great beginning.

"Mama!" Teddy almost fell in the enthusiasm to get to her.

"Come on, Daddy you need to walk faster," she teased.

Teddy stopped and tipped his head back to look at Kent. "Dada."

Kent's proud smile was bigger than life. His smile was contagious.

"Looks like I missed all the excitement. Oh, Teddy I'm so delighted! What a big boy you are." She set down her bag and swept Teddy up giving him kisses on his cheeks, neck and belly. His laughter made her day.

"I have lunch ready," Kent told her.

She blinked. "Really? Wonderful, I'm starving!" She walked over to Kent and tilted her head so he could kiss her. There was nothing better than her husband's kiss.

"Here give Teddy to me. You're supposed to be resting that arm."

Dutifully she handed Teddy over and followed them into the house. "I forgot my bag."

"Stay put I'll get it."

The table was set and the plates each had a sandwich on it. It looked good. So far she hadn't had to cook a thing. She'd have to confess her ineptness soon. Kent came back in with her bag but he didn't appear happy.

"Why the frown?" she asked.

"I guess there was trouble on the road leading to the ranch"

"What kind of trouble?"

"Crumb said it looked to be all the men in town. They protested that Parker was giving good jobs to the freedmen and paying them a fair wage."

She furrowed her brow. "What's wrong with that?"

"They claim that white men should have been given the jobs and housing." Kent sat at the table. "We never could find enough reliable white men to fill the jobs. We need to find out who is riling these men up."

Glory sat at the table with Teddy on her lap. She pulled his sandwich apart into smaller pieces.

Kent stood and took Teddy from her. "Doesn't your shoulder hurt?" He sat with Teddy on his lap and fed him.

"It aches and since it was my fault I don't feel I'm able to complain. School went well. There were armed cowboys there, but it went well. I met a Mrs. Harkins. Did you know two of her boys were sold when they were just babies? I can't imagine it."

"Not to defend the owners but it was their way of life for well over a hundred years. They were brought up to believe the slaves were property not people. People find it hard to change and many are still bitter over the war. Cotton was huge money making crop here in Texas and if the plantation owners had to pay their workers, it would cut into the profits. We went through a period where the slave owners called slavery apprenticeships to get around federal law. You don't have to pay an apprentice if you give them food and lodging."

"That's horrible! I'm glad Parker built houses and gave them jobs." She took a bite of her sandwich. "I appreciate you making lunch."

"Anytime darling," He drawled.

"I do so like your southern accent."

He grinned at her. "Really? Your accent just sounds funny."

Her jaw dropped as he laughed. Teddy laughed too. "Ganging up on me are you?"

"Yes, Ma'am."

"Well, when you two are done with lunch, it's naptime."

Kent winked at her. "Now would this include you too?"

Her face heated as her lips twitched. "I have work to do."

"Unfortunately, I have a few horses to train or I'd make you rest for a while."

KENT PUT Teddy on the bed and tucked him in and after he walked back into the main room, he took Glory carefully into his arms. "When do you think we'll have a wedding night?"

She put her head against his chest. "When my shoulder heals and after you build a trundle bed for Teddy."

She felt so soft and so right in his arms. "I'll get on making the bed. You be sure to rest that arm."

He tilted his head and placed a soft kiss on her lips and then another. Her small groan encouraged him and he deepened the kiss. He never felt this way with any other woman. Just touching her made him tingle all over. He pulled away before he went too far with her. The rosy color of her cheeks made him smile. "You like it when I kiss you."

"You can stop grinning like that. Maybe I do and maybe I don't." She stared at his shirt instead of making eye contact.

"By the pink color of your cheeks, I'd say you liked it. There was also a little groan you made—"

She took a step away from him putting more distance between them. Then she smoothed down her dress and touched her hair with one hand before she stared at him. "A lady doesn't groan and if she did, I would think it would be polite if the gentleman didn't mention it."

The sides of his mouth began to curl upwards. "So I'm not supposed to mention the groan that made me believe you yearned for my kisses?"

She put on what he figured to be her no nonsense teacher's face. "I believe the word yearning is a bit strong in this case."

"Oh, you do?" He closed the distance between them and kissed her again. As soon as she groaned he stopped. "See did you hear that? It was a groan of yearning."

She bit her bottom lip, and he suspected it was to keep from laughing. "You have a nice imagination."

"Unfortunately darlin', I have work to do. Don't miss me too much. Lock the door after me." He whistled when he put on his hat and left.

"About time you came to help," Willis teased. "Being married has made you a dilly dallier of the worst kind."

"Oh, do you still work here?" Max asked.

"I had to watch Teddy while my wife taught school. We'll find someone to watch him soon enough."

"You've taken to marriage like a duck takes to water. I'm happy for you, Sandler," Max said.

"It looks you two have been jawin' out here all morning. Where are we on breaking the horses?"

"While you were changing diapers, Max and me, we got them all broke. Now we have to train them. These quarter horses will make us rich!" Willis smiled.

"I heard there was trouble by the road today."

Willis and Max nodded.

Willis frowned. "What I want to know is how do they know every move we make around here? Someone must have told them that your wife was teaching today."

"We need to keep our eyes open and keep everyone safe," Max added.

"Yes, we do. How's Walter?" Kent asked.

"He's doing real well. He wanted to come and work with us today but Sondra won't let him," Max said with a snicker.

Kent nodded. "I'm glad he's healing well."

"Listen, Sandler, Veronica feels awful about the way she treated Glory."

"Maybe she could come by and have tea or whatever women do. Glory feels hurt and friendless over the whole thing. She's bewildered why Sondra took such a dislike of her."

Max clapped Kent's shoulder. "I'll tell Veronica. She's

been feeling alone too. She has Bridey but an adult friend would be good for her."

Willis picked up a lead rope. "While you two plan a tea party, I've got work to do." He walked to the pasture.

Kent laughed. "He'll feel differently when he gets married." He took two lead ropes and tossed one to Max.

"He claims he doesn't want a wife but we'll see. Now, tell me the story of how Glory stabbed herself. I can't seem to make sense of it."

Kent laughed as they walked to the pasture. "It's a hard one to make sense of."

———

GLORY'S FACE was still hot long after Kent left. Yearning? If having your stomach all jumpy, your heart racing, and wanting to be closer to him than kissing, maybe he was right. She liked the sight of him too. He was a handsome one. After all, he apologized about saying she wasn't Teddy's mother. Oh, how that had hurt. Now her heart just seemed to grow and fill. It was unlike anything she'd ever felt or imagined.

She glanced over at her sewing pile and frowned. Once her shoulder healed, it was time to tell him how inadequate she was. Maybe Georgie had a cookbook. Cooking had to be the same as making healing potions. And she practiced hemming more diapers and she'd figure it out.

When she was able, she was going into the woods with Kent and see what she could find for her concoctions. She so missed her school mates. They always told her she could do something when she had doubts. Glory wanted to reach out to Veronica, but she didn't know what to say. She could picture herself mumbling and then having all thoughts leave her head. She wanted to meet Veronica and Max's little girl Bridey.

"Mama!"

She hurried into the bedroom remembering that she was supposed to rest. Changing a diaper with one good arm would be a challenge.

"Hello my big boy. You ready to get up? First, we need to change you." He smiled up at her.

Getting the wet diaper off and washing him clean wasn't hard but putting a fresh one was exhausting. Teddy thought it to be fun to roll this way and that way and squirm laughing all the while. It took a long while, but she finally got the diaper on him and she set him on the floor.

As quick as a racing stallion he crawled into the kitchen. He sat on the floor and looked at her expectantly.

"Are you hungry? Yes?"

Teddy nodded and said "No!"

"You want nothing to eat?"

"No!"

"Do you know what no means?"

"No!"

She burst out laughing. "It's fine you're learning how to say new words. That's where it all starts." Reaching into a wide-mouthed jar, she picked out a cookie and handed it to him. "Is this what you want?"

He smiled as he reached for it. "No!" He took it from her and ate it all by himself.

"I think you mean yes but we'll work on it."

Teddy finished his cookie leaving a good amount of crumbs behind. He crawled to her and pulled himself up to a standing position and held on to her skirts.

"Look at you! I can hardly keep up with all the changes. You are a smart, strong, sweet boy. I love you so much!"

He giggled. "Love."

Tears filled her eyes. He probably didn't know what the word meant, but she didn't care. He was making so much progress in such a short time. He'd be sitting in the class-room in a couple years. She still needed someone to watch Teddy while she taught. Did Kent make enough money for them to hire someone? No one mentioned she'd be getting any salary. She'd do it anyway, but she needed to ask Kent about it.

Glass shattered, and she grabbed Teddy as she dove for the ground. This time it was a bullet. Another shot hit the fireplace and then another hit the wall. Time slowed, and she had Teddy crawl with her into the bedroom.

There was a pistol and bullets on top of the wardrobe. She had Teddy stay down as she tried to reach. Her stitches popped. The pain was excruciating but Teddy's safety came first. Whoever was out there could climb through the window and get to them. She reached again and could grab both the gun and the ammunition.

She'd watched the men put bullets in their guns. It looked easy. She studied the gun and couldn't figure out how to open it. She knew she needed to cock the thing on the top back and pull the trigger. Point and shoot? It felt heavy in her hand, it must be loaded. She slipped out of the bedroom, closing the door behind her. Teddy's cry was hard to listen to.

She stayed down and scanned the house. No one else was in it. After sighing in relief she crawled to the sofa and peered over it at the window.

Another shot came through and she thought it hit the sofa. She gulped hard. Her hands shook as she reached the gun up over her head, above the sofa back and she squeezed the trigger. Nothing happened. She forgot to pull back the top thing. She quickly did that and put the gun up again and pulled the trigger.

The kick of the gun kocked her back. She knew she hit the wall and missed the window completely. The gun was loaded. Everything was eerily quiet for a few minutes and then the door was kicked in. All she wanted to do was go back into the bedroom, grab Teddy and hide under the bed with her eyes closed.

She cocked the gun again and waiting behind the couch. She'd have to be close to the man if she would hit him with a bullet.

"Glory? Glory it's me!" Kent called out.

She wanted to answer, but something froze her right where she was. Teddy continued to cry. She had to protect Teddy. She put her finger on the trigger and she shot aiming for the window again. She heard the bullet hit wood again.

"Glory! Stop shooting!" Kent rounded the sofa.

She knew she was safe but she couldn't let go of the gun but she didn't cock it either. Kent approached her slowly on his knees and took the gun from her. He kissed her cheek and left to get Teddy.

This house wasn't safe. It was cursed. She couldn't stay in it. "Are they gone?"

"By the time we got there they were gone. They used rifles so they could have been a good distance away when they shot."

She stared at Kent and Teddy as she stood up. Willis and Max startled a yell out of her when they came into view. She had to get out of there. With a strangled cry she rushed to the door and went outside.

She gulped in the fresh air feeling unable to get enough to breathe. Leaning against the house she wrapped her arm around herself and slightly rocked back and forth. How could she live and raise children here? There was too much violence. She'd used up all her bravery and now she was scared witless.

She turned away from others who came onto the porch. She wasn't up to much more than crying and she was doing her best not to. She felt someone touch her arm, and she jumped before she turned her head.

"I'm so sorry about all the trouble you've been having," Veronica said.

Glory nodded, but it wasn't Veronica that piqued her interest it was her baby girl.

"Her name is Bridey."

"Can I hold her?" Glory asked shyly. When Veronica nodded, Glory sat down on the bench and held out her arm. "She's so beautiful."

Glory examined her little nose and smile and then held her up against her shoulder. Holding the baby calmed Glory even if it was awkward with one arm. "Her features are all so petite. It makes me miss the orphanage. There were always so many babies and when I wasn't hiding out and reading, I was rocking the babies. I've seen many but none as beautiful as this little angel."

"She is a pretty baby," Veronica agreed. "Mind if I sit down?"

"Please do."

Veronica sat next to her on the bench. "I admire you and the work you are doing. I grew up poorer than poor and it was a daily struggle to get my Pa to let me go to school. He thought education was wasted on a girl. I'm glad I fought to go now I have Bridey it's important to share my knowledge and when she goes to school, I can look over her homework or help her if needed."

"That's admirable. I never thought there was an attitude that education is wasted on a girl. I suppose with so much work that needs to be done around homesteads it might be a common attitude."

"It was. It determined me to be someone and to make something out of my life. It was a long, long road but I'm here with Max who is so sweet and kind and Bridey."

"There she goes again telling people I'm sweet again. I used to get people to back down with just a look but not anymore. They all think I'm sweet," Max said in mock distress.

Veronica laughed. "Would you rather I tell people you are rattlesnake mean?"

"It might help my reputation if you told a few people." He smiled widely at Veronica. Their love was there for all to see.

Max suddenly grew somber. "Glory are you all right? It must have been scary as h… very scary. Hear tell you had a pistol, and you were shooting back. Good for you."

Glory's face heated. "I've never held a gun before. I think I hit every wall in our house."

"It was enough to scare them away. Kent will teach you to shoot. Do you know how to ride?" Max said.

"A horse?"

He chuckled. "Yes, a horse. It's the form of transportation around here and everyone should know how to saddle one and ride one."

"That is worthy advice, Max, thank you."

Kent approached them with Teddy in his arms. "I see you've met the fair Bridey. And Max is right. Tomorrow after school we'll start our lessons on shooting and riding."

"What will we do with Teddy while we do that?" She asked quietly.

"I'll be happy to have him at my house," Veronica offered. "It'll be easy as long as they both crawl in the same direction."

Glory laughed. Veronica was a nice woman. Kent must have been right about how she was treated after someone shot Walter. They were in a panic and they didn't know her. Glory had always been supersensitive to what anyone said or did.

There would be no shooting or riding with the way her shoulder hurt but she'd let Kent know later.

She studied Teddy as he laid his head on Kent's strong shoulders. She caught Kent's gaze and cocked her right brow. Kent slowly shook his head and stroked Teddy's back.

"I probably should take Teddy inside and make sure he feels safe. It was a nightmare for us both but I had to put Teddy in the bedroom and close the door. His cries pierced my heart, but I had no other choice. I was afraid with the window shattered that the shooter could get into the house." She handed Bridey back to Veronica and stood.

"Thanks for coming by to check on me. We'll bring Teddy by tomorrow before my cowgirl lessons," she smiled. She saw Georgie coming across but Glory was too weary to visit anymore. "Tell Georgie I'll visit with her in a while."

She took Teddy from Kent and headed inside the house. The sight of the shattered window was too much. She hurried into the bedroom, closed the door and sat Teddy on her lap facing her.

"You are the bravest boy I know. You know Mama loves you don't you? I'm sorry I had to leave you in the room alone."

He grasped the material of her dress near her aching shoulder and pulled himself closer to her. She pulled him closer and held him as tight. His tears soaked through her dress. It occurred to her he wasn't making a sound, tears were just pouring out of his eyes. Before she knew it she was doing the same.

She lay on the bed with him in her arms. It killed her he was crying like that but she also knew there wasn't anything she could do but make him feel safe again.

The bedroom door opened and Kent came in. He got on the bed and spooned her and wrapped his arms around them both. "It will be fine. I'm so sorry I left you defenseless. I'm not sure I'd be able to go on if I lost either of you."

Teddy instantly calmed, and she felt safer in Kent's arms.

He kissed the side of her neck sending delicious chills through her. "I've decided that I like you," she teased.

"Oh? I wasn't aware that you were deciding. After all everyone likes me. But I'm glad you decided in my favor." There was humor in his voice.

"There has been a moment here and there when I didn't know if I should stay. But I don't want to leave. So much has happened since I got here. I'm used to a well-ordered life where I know where I'm supposed to be at any given time. It can be chaotic here and I feel overwhelmed. I'm used to Imogene, Harriet and Fae being by my side. The most danger I was ever in, was being caught reading my botany books when I was supposed to be in cooking class. I need to go into town. I have a few letters to post and I'd like to see Spring Water. I know you have your work to do but maybe sometime we could go."

He kissed her neck again. "I'll always find time for you. I have to confess I like you too. I also wondered if you would cut and run. It can be violent in Texas but I think most of the southern states are experiencing the same if not worse. The West is full of hardship and danger too. There are outlaws and Indians. I know there is always work that needs to be done but we'll never be in danger of starving. But there is plenty to look forward to. The new school, watching Teddy to learn to walk and maybe someday we can have a baby of our own."

She stiffened at the last part.

"You don't want to have children?"

Too bad she couldn't turn and look him in the eye. "I want children. Your children, Kent. I'm afraid of making them is all." Closing her eyes, she waited for him to pull away.

"Perhaps we've let postponing our wedding night go on

too long. It's a beautiful expression of love if you have the right person."

"Is that what the key is, the right person? I've heard it was a duty, and it hurt and women dreaded it and only certain types of women like it."

He kissed the back of her neck this time. "First, pleasure does not make one a soiled dove. It makes for an extra happy husband. I suppose someone could look it as a duty if it's a chore to you. I think I can make it so you'll want to do it again and again." He ran his hand from her waist to her thigh and up again and she trembled.

"I think it's the wanting that makes a woman wanton. A good pious woman would not have desires."

"Is that what you want to be, Glory? I wonder if a pious woman has a lick of fun? I feel you tremble under my touch. That's part of wanting. Does that make you a bad person?"

"Maybe. It makes me wish we were alone so I could have one of your kisses. I shouldn't have said that. I don't know what I'm supposed to say or not say or how to act. I think we should just do it and get it over with and that will be the end." She felt him laughing silently. "What's so funny?"

He stroked her side again, and it was making so she could hardly think.

"It's not a onetime thing. It's something that is done throughout a marriage. Tell you what, let's keep working on our kissing and we'll get there."

She relaxed against him. "I like kissing." She yawned.

"Teddy's already asleep. Why don't you sleep for? I want to get the window boarded up and talk to Parker and the men."

"I like you, Glory Sandler." He kissed her cheek before he got up and left.

His warmth was missed.

CHAPTER NINE

*K*ent was the first to wake the next morning and the first thought in his mind was of Glory and her odd notions about making love. He smiled, she sure was something! They really need a night alone so he could put all of her worries to rest. He'd just kiss her every chance he got.

He got the stove put on the coffee. Glory hadn't showed off her cooking skills and now with her shoulder he'd have to wait. He should have checked her injury last night.

He would find out who was trying to kill his family. It didn't sit well with him they could get close enough to his house. Who was on guard duty yesterday? He wanted to tell Glory no more teaching but that wouldn't be fair to anyone. It wasn't right when a man's family wasn't safe in their own house.

In the military they would have hunted the man or men down. Those tactics aren't allowed in a civilized world. Perhaps they all needed to spend more time in town to figure out who the Pale-Faces were. The hooded men had a name.

He went into the bedroom and there was Teddy smiling

at him. "Dada! Eat?" Kent's heart wanted to explode with each new word. "Yes eat. First, we'll get you changed and dressed."

"Mama! Mama!"

"Shh. Let your mama sleep."

"Mama is already awake." Glory sat up in bed with her long dark hair cascading all around her. "I can't believe I slept in my dress."

"I want to look at your shoulder before you get dressed."

Guilt crossed her face. "What happened?"

"I tore the stitches yesterday." She unbuttoned the top of her dress and looked at her shoulder. "Looks like I must have it stitched up again."

"I think you've set a record here on the ranch. I remember no one having to have the same wound stitches up three times. I will make breakfast and then tend to you."

She nodded, and he swooped down and kissed her. It was a light kiss but there would be plenty more. He liked the light blush that covered her skin. This kissing thing might be fun. He changed Teddy and then dressed him.

"Come on, little man. I think we'll see if you like eggs and bacon. Glory the coffee is ready. You might as well wait to get cleaned up until after I fix those stitches."

She sighed and then studied him. "Just how many people have you stitched up?"

"A few."

"Enough to know what you're doing?" Her brows furrowed as she frowned.

"You're in good hands." He handed her a mug. "Drink some of that bark tree."

She snickered. "It's willow bark tea."

"Like I said good hands." He began to gather what was needed trying not to laugh at the worried expression on her face. He'd stitched up plenty of men in the army. He'd even take his time, so she didn't end up with a jagged scar.

Finally he was ready. He put everything on the table and made sure Teddy was busy with his blocks. "You'll need to unbutton your gown and pull your arm out of your sleeve."

She hesitated for a moment and then did it. Her eyes widened when he got closer. Her stomach fluttered and fear clung to her at the same time. "It will hurt," she whispered.

"That's why I made you that willow tree tea." Isn't it working?"

"Just be gentle."

He smiled and kissed her cheek. "I will always be gentle." He caught her gaze and held it as she fussed with her gown making sure she was as covered as possible. Finally she nodded.

He took the scissors and made sure that all the thread from last time was gone. He poured whiskey on a cloth and held it against her shoulder. She didn't flinch, but she hissed. Next he stitched her up. Sewing wasn't easy. He was trying to be neat so her scar wouldn't be hideous. She grimaced a few times. Finally he was done.

"Do you want some comfy paste?"

"Comfrey," she corrected.

"That's what I said." He reached into a cupboard and pulled the jar down. "I can put it on you if it'll make it easier for you."

Glory nodded. "Yes, please then a bandage to cover it. I have children to teach soon."

He opened the jar expecting it to smell bad, but it didn't. After he spread it all over, he made sure it was nicely covered with a bandage.

"Thank you. I appreciate all you've done."

"I'd say anytime but I really don't want to stitch you up again. No lifting, no chasing outlaws." He tried to make light of the situation but from the look on her face he didn't succeed.

"You'll be fine. Crumb and Monty will guard you and the children today."

"I don't remember Monty. Have I met him?"

"You'd remember if you'd met him. He is a string bean thin with red hair and freckles. You can't miss him."

"I'll get dressed and then we can go." She stood and gingerly touched her bandage and winced."

"We can cancel if you like?"

Glory shook her head. "I'll be fine."

GLORY WAS SO pleased to see the children all coming to join her under the tree. They all looked eager to learn, mostly. There were a few of the older boys that never looked happy.

"Good morning. Sit down so we can get started." She let the children get comfortable on the grass. "Let's see how much we remember about the alphabet. What's the first letter?"

"A," most of the class said.

Glory smiled. Her leg itched something bad, and she tried to pretend to fix her skirt so she could lean over and scratch it. Looking down, she saw an enormous amount of tiny ants that looked to be red. She'd never seen them before. They were all over her shoes.

Next she heard a few of the children scream and saw red ants everywhere including on the children. They jumped up and tried to brush the ants off but from the noise they weren't making much headway.

"Children come away from there." She hurried to an open spot where she saw none. "Try to help each other and get the ants off you."

The itching and burning was traveling up her thigh. Oh, my! "Do these ants bite?"

"They sure do, Miss Glory. It's best we go on home," Hannah said. "They are under our clothes too."

"Yes, yes, get those ants off you. We'll figure something out for tomorrow." She stood in her spot until each child was on the trail home.

Then she made a run for it. She ran right into Kent. "Red ants. They are biting my thighs."

"Stay here." He ran inside and came back with a towel. Kneeling he took the towel and wiped the ants off of her shoes and ankles. "I will have to lift your skirt."

"I don't care if they go any higher…"

Kent started to slowly lift her skirts, but she jerked her skirt up showing her platelets covered thighs. The ants were swarming.

"Darling I will have to pull these off you."

"Do it!"

Kent untied the ribbon that held the pantalets up and quickly had them off of her. He threw her under garment onto the porch and grabbed the towel, wiping away the ants. Finally he took her hand and led her into the house.

"Stay next to the door. I need to get everything off you starting with your shoes."

Her face had paled, but she nodded. He took off one item at a time, threw it out the doors and used the towel to get rid of the ants. He made sure he killed them as they fell. Finally he took off her chemise.

She quickly used her one arm to cover herself.

"Stand still so I can see if I got them all" If the circumstances had been different he would have enjoyed the view. He got all the remaining ants off of her and told her to put on a nightgown. He'd have to put something on all the bites.

She ran into the bedroom and quickly covered herself.

Oh, the bites stung something awful. Hopefully, her students fared better.

"Basil leaves! Kent, ask Georgie for the leaves. I can make the paste. I bet Letty is taking care of the children. I hope there are enough leaves for everyone."

Kent nodded and hurried out the door while Teddy crawled to her. He pulled himself up and stood next to the bed.

"My what a big boy you are Teddy!"

"Teddy big boy," he said. Then he tried to climb on the bed. She helped him with her good arm and then lay next to him. Tears filled her eyes. Partly from the bites but also because Teddy was making huge strides every day.

He lay there and smiled at her. Then he put his head on her stomach and fell asleep as she stroked his hair.

Kent came home and quietly looked into the bedroom. He smiled. "Georgia has basil growing behind her house. She planted it I guess. Anyway, I have to grind up the leaves and add water. I'll be right back."

The poor children. It was strange that there were so many ants suddenly.

Kent walked back in with a bowl in his hand. He set it down on the table next to the bed. "Since you're occupied, I'll put it on you. You need not turn so red. I've already seen you."

"It's embarrassing. That is why I turn red."

"You've never been with a man that's why." He lifted her gown and worked from her thighs to her feet. It felt good going on.

"How are the children?" she whispered.

"Letty and Georgie are tending to them. Letty grows basil too. Lots of unhappy kids though."

"I figured as much. I know nothing about those vicious red ants. They weren't there yesterday."

"I know. From what Sondra said, someone dug up an ant colony and set it by the tree and then sprinkled sugar all around. We have a rat around here and we need to figure out who it is."

"Kent, do you think the rat shot at the house?"

"I wouldn't rule it out. We don't know where every man is though we will take note of who is with what group and who seems to be missing. The ranch is huge, and we split up into groups to get everything done. We'll figure it out. I'm just mad that you and the children had to suffer."

"I'm surprised that none of the mothers were there today."

"Sadie is in labor and from what I hear the first one can take a while."

"I'm glad she has so much help."

"That's why Georgie went to Joy. She's tending to the children whose mothers are helping with the birth. Most have been bitten before but not to the magnitude of today."

"Someone really doesn't want me to teach the children. I must think about it. It might be better if I stayed home with Teddy." Her heart ached. She promised Madam Wigg she'd teach.

"I need to post a few letters. Can we go into town tomorrow?" She met his gaze and saw his uncertainty.

"I can't teach you to shoot with that shoulder of yours. I'll talk to Parker and make sure they can spare me tomorrow." He leaned down and kissed her lips. It started as a light kiss but then it progressed into a kiss that made her feel things she'd never felt before.

He stood up and stared into her eyes. "Are you all right?"

"I, well, I, hm, I never felt this way before. I'm sure what I felt was desire. It's unsettling yet I enjoyed the kiss."

Kent gave her a wide grin. "Desire, huh? Then it was superb kiss indeed. Get some rest. I'm going back to work."

She couldn't hide her smile, even after he left. Her stomach fluttered, and she wanted him to keep kissing her. It was a good thing he'd explained some of this to her or she'd be feeling shamed but there wasn't anything to be ashamed of.

She almost fell asleep when she remembered the door was unlocked. Carefully she shifted Teddy and eased out of bed. Then she padded across the floor and locked the door. She glanced at the boarded window in the main room and shook her head. They'd have no windows if the outlaws had their way. No, that wasn't right they weren't exactly outlaws someone called them Pale-Faces. Did they think they were whiter than most? Kent wouldn't be allowed. He sometimes took his shirt off when he worked and the sun had darkened his skin to a golden color.

She couldn't and wouldn't let Madam Wigg down. She'd taken such good care of them all from the first. Glory had been an infant when she was left at the orphanage. Madam Wigg had been like a mother to her and Glory missed her. She'd probably say *Glory there is nothing to be afraid of. Stand up straight with your shoulders back and remember you are a wonderful girl.* Then she'd say- *Off with you now. Join the other girls.*

Glory sighed as she climbed back into bed. The bites still hurt, but they didn't burn as much.

Before she knew it, Teddy was tapping her head and saying *Mama.*

Glory smiled. "Did you sleep well?"

"Door, Mama."

For a moment it confused her until she heard the knocking. She helped Teddy out of the bed as best she could and went to open the door.

"Heavy sleeper," Kent remarked. He walked into the house and locked the door behind him.

"Just how long have you been out there?"

He shook his head. "You don't want to know."

"That long? Teddy just woke me."

"I could hear Teddy calling you but it took a while for you to wake up." Kent wrapped his arms around her and kissed her lips again.

It wasn't as good as the kiss before. This time she had Teddy tugging on her skirt. Glory laughed. "He really needs to be changed if you don't mind."

"I don't mind." Kent bent over and lifted Teddy up. "I know what you mean Teddy. Women always want a man to be clean and fresh."

Glory laughed. She was grateful that her husband was someone she could love. Love? Where had that thought come from? No, she wouldn't risk her heart she was too sensitive and it would lead to no good.

She wished she could make bread. Kneading the dough was good for getting out her frustrations. She hated her bandage on her shoulder. When was it going to heal up? She sat on the sofa and almost laughed at herself. She already knew the answer. Not any time soon if she kept tearing the stitches.

"Kent, do you think I can shake out my clothes from earlier? I hate leaving them on the porch."

Kent came out of the bedroom with a smiling Teddy in his arms. "They aren't out there anymore. Sondra and Veronica have a big tub over a fire and they're boiling the clothes to make sure the ants are dead."

"They had to go to so much trouble just because of those pesky ants?"

"Yes, and when they change the water they pour the hot water where the ants were."

"Could you make me a cup of willow bark tea?"

"I can."

She laughed. "Look at me ordering you around."

"You'd do the same for me."

"Of course," she said without hesitation.

"Once I get you situated I will see about going into town tomorrow."

"I'd like that."

CHAPTER TEN

The sun was out and there was a nice cooling breeze as Kent drove the wagon. He glanced over his shoulder. "You two all right back there?"

"It's bumpy but I think we'll survive," Glory responded.

Kent chuckled to himself. Glory had tried to climb up onto the wagon seat by herself with one arm. He'd put his hands on her waist and lifted her down. She started to protest, but he kissed her speechless. Then Teddy wanted a kiss from her.

Kent then showed her the back with the quilts rolled up to keep them from hitting the sides of the wooden wagon. He had to admit he had smiled little before Glory. How did she really think she'd be able to hold on to her seat and Teddy with one good arm?

He found his desire for her growing quickly. At first he thought he could wait forever, it made no difference to him but as he got to know her, well, his heart quickened whenever he was near her and kissing her made him yearn for her something fierce. It was a great sign the way she reacted to his kisses. Now with her shoulder he'd have to wait even longer. Maybe he could make the anticipation of the wedding night grow in Glory as it had inside him.

He halted the team and jumped down. "Need to hide my gun, I'll be right back." He went behind a big bolder where they all their firearms from the Yankees. They didn't allow guns in town. He wanted the Yankees gone in the worst way but he might have need after all.

He hopped back up and drove to the checkpoint at the edge of town. Just his luck Sergeant Hollanda was there. He was a big windbag and a pain in the neck.

"Sandler, who is in the wagon?" Sergeant Hollanda walked to the back and stared at Glory and Teddy and then frowned.

"I have my wife and son with me. We'd like to go shopping."

Hollanda narrowed his eyes at Kent. "Cause none of your Johnny Reb trouble."

Kent clenched his jaw and urged the horses forward. He parked the wagon right outside the general store. He set the brake and hurried to help Glory and his son down. Carrying Teddy, he noticed that Glory wore the same dress she'd arrived in. Perhaps he needed to help with the laundry when they got home. He suddenly realized Glory had gotten blood on some of her new dresses.

He held the door open for Glory and followed her inside. "Morning, Stack," he called out to the young man behind the counter. Kent always wondered why Anson Stack never married.

"Morning, Sandler." Anson came out into the store.

"This is my wife Glory and my son Teddy."

Anson smiled. "It's a pleasure to meet you ma'am and you too Teddy."

Glory gave him a regal nod. "It's nice to meet you too and please call me Glory."

"Glory it is. Teddy looks so normal you'd never know he had something wrong with his brain. Poor kid but at least he has you two."

Kent glared for a moment and then took a deep breath. "Where'd you hear that from?"

"The whole town knows. Don't worry no one will tease him."

Glory's hand went to her chest as an expression of worry crossed her face.

"Teddy do you like the store?"

Teddy nodded and pointed at a small toy wagon. "For me, Dada." Teddy smiled proudly.

There was joy on Glory's face. "He talks more and more every day. I'm just amazed at how quickly he learns."

Anson's face reddened. "I must have heard the wrong story."

"Seems to happen often in towns and Spring Water is no exception. Teddy is my and my late wife's son. He lived with his grandmother who fed him but left him in the crib most of the time. They never informed me that I had a son until my former mother-in-law dropped him off at the wedding. He didn't know how to talk or crawl. He's catching on fast." Kent ruffled Teddy's hair. "Yes, you can have the wagon." He squatted down with Teddy in his arms and allowed Teddy to pick out the wagon. The joy on his son's face made everything worth it.

"I like the truth much better. Now how can I help you?"

"I have a few letters to post," Glory said. She reached into her pocket and pulled the letters out.

"Come on back to the counter with me and I can take care of it for you."

They all followed Anson to the back counter and Glory handed him the letters.

"Is there anything else?" Kent asked her.

"No, I wanted to mail these."

"We'll take the wagon and however much the postage is."

Glory wandered away looking at the goods. When she was out of earshot Kent asked Anson to also include three peppermint sticks.

When he finished paying, they said goodbye to Anson and left the store.

"It's a pretty town. It's very quiet. Is there a place where the freedmen live? I want to see if anyone had any knowledge of Lucy and Anthony's two boys."

Kent hesitated. It might just make them bigger targets. There was so much hope in her eyes he couldn't deny her. "It's this way."

They walked to the opposite end of the town where shacks stood. They looked as though a good wind could knock them all over. There was an elderly woman in a rocking chair who smiled at them.

"So young miss, I hear you're a rabble rouser. I say good for you. It gladdens my heart to know those children are learning."

Glory smiled. "Thank you. I enjoy it. I wanted to ask if anyone here knew anything about James and his brother Manor. They might have taken the last name Roebuck. Their parents Anthony and Lucy Harkins kive on the ranch."

"they sold away Their children from them." The older woman shook her head. "I know a few Roebucks. Of course, I'll have to wait until the end of the workday to ask but I'll pass the information on. There are so many people looking for their families. It breaks my heart. But you go on now and I'll see what I can do."

"Thank you…"

"Adelle is my name."

"I'm Glory."

"We know your name. You've given people hope that we'll all have a future someday."

"It was nice to meet you." Glory said as she tucked her good hand into the crook of Kent's bent elbow.

They walked and Kent could feel people watching them. It was uncomfortable. "One more stop, then we can go."

He stopped in front of the sheriff's office and went in. It was filled with Union Soldiers sitting around. Everything went silent when they entered.

"Major Cooke, I'd like a moment of your time."

"What do you want, Sandler?" The major took his feet off the desk and sat up straight.

"We've had a lot happen at the ranch. Shooting at my wife and child is high on the list."

"Did you see who did it?" The major crossed his arms in front of him.

"No, and we have doubled our guards, but it hasn't deterred whoever is causing the problems."

Out of the corner of his eye he saw Glory walk to the wall and read the wanted poster. She turned pale and looked as though she was ready to pass out.

"I wanted you to know. Come, Glory we need to get back home."

She seemed scared. "Yes, I'd like that." She flung open the door and hurried outside. Her gait was fast as she walked to the wagon.

Kent had to hurry to catch up with her. "Glory, what happened in there?"

"There's a wanted poster, and the picture looks just like my friend Xenia. The name was different, but it sure looked like her. She's wanted for robbing a train. They called the thief Mad Mary. Kent I'm afraid for her."

"There's nothing you can do. I'm sure if she was in trouble she'd go back to the school and get help."

"Yes you're right." She waited while he lifted Teddy into the wagon and then he lifted her. Somehow she didn't seem at all convinced. Glory said a silent prayer for all the girls that became mail-order brides and teachers.

He jumped up onto the seat and turned the wagon toward the way they came. No one bothered him when they left and then he stopped to collect his gun.

"We'll be home soon."

Home it was such a simple word, but it filled her with emotion. It was nice to have a home to go to and the joy of having a family. Teddy played with his wagon with a big smile on his face. He was so different from the boy they'd gotten not long ago.

As soon as her shoulder healed, she would learn to shoot. She needed to protect her child.

"What's put that delightful smile on your face?" Kent asked as he glanced back at her.

"Everything. Having a home to go to. Being married to such a kind man and being a mother. My life is nothing like I'd imagined but it's much better than what I thought."

"Don't forget good looking, strong, a hard worker, a good father and the best kisser in all of Texas." He chuckled.

"Maybe some of that is true," she conceded.

He glanced over his shoulder again. "I know which one you mean and I plan to prove it to you as soon as we get a private moment."

She swore he hit every bump on the trail. She'd be one sore woman when she got home. That was another thing that had changed. She'd always thought of herself as a girl but she was a woman.

"We probably should see about a trundle bed for the little one," she said loudly.

"On it."

She waited, but he didn't elaborate. She'd find out later. They still needed to figure out what to do about school. She wanted to continue but only if they had a safe place. Out in the pasture with the cattle would be the best place. She smiled. The children would probably want to ride them.

"That's a great wagon, Teddy."

He glanced up and nodded. "Dada give me it." He showed her how the wheels worked. "Me like Dada." He pointed to the wagon and then at Kent.

"Yes, you'll grow up to be big and strong and smart like your dada. Your brain seems to be at the right level for your age. It's the communication and few other things."

Teddy slid over and crawled into her lap. "My mama."

Her heart squeezed as she stroked his dark hair. He was the image of Kent. They had Teddy now, and that was all that mattered.

They arrived home and Kent helped them both down. "I have to take care of the horses and the wagon and I think I should put in some time working with the quarter horses. I earn my keep."

She nodded and Kent stood toe to toe with her. He swooped down and kissed her enough to leave her shaky. "I told you my kisses were the best." He grinned and walked toward the horses.

He sure knew how to make her heart flutter. She wished she could let Lucy know Adelle would put the word out about James and Manor but there wasn't any way for her to carry Teddy. She'd get a message to her somehow.

They went into the house and she locked the door behind her. Then she grabbed the shotgun, made sure it was loaded and put it in the middle of the table where Teddy couldn't reach it. After that she took her bloodstained gowns and sighed. The blood hadn't come out. She wasn't left with many dresses to wear. She stared at the pile of cut out material and wished she could sew but not with the way her shoulder was.

There was a knock on the door and it surprised Glory to see Sondra.

"Hello Sondra, would you care to come in?"

"No, thank you. Georgie sent me. She's having Veronica and Bridey over for tea and would like you and Teddy to join her." Sondra looked everywhere except at Glory.

"I'd be delighted. Thank you for coming to invite me." Glory smiled trying to convey that bygones were bygones but Sondra didn't seem to want to. In fact, she turned and left without another word.

It was Sondra's problem now. Glory would just act as if nothing was wrong. She went to the bedroom and brushed her hair. She bemoaned that there was so much material waiting to be sewn into dresses for her. She'd figure something out.

She changed Teddy and then walked across the yard to Georgie's house with him in her arm. I delighted Glory in the big hug she got from both Georgie and Veronica. Sondra looked to be absent.

Both Douglas and Bridey were standing at the table near the couch, holding on. As soon as Teddy was put down, he crawled to the table and did the same thing.

"Isn't that cute?" Georgie asked. "Come sit down I feel as though we have had little time to talk with everything going on around here." She led the way and motioned for her two guests to sit on the sofa while she sat in a chair across from them. By then the children had crawled over to the toys and played.

"How's your shoulder, Glory," Veronica asked.

"Unfortunately Kent had to restitch me. I pulled them out trying to shoot a rifle."

"Oh, that must have hurt. Did he do a good job?" Georgie asked.

"Actually, I was surprised how small and neat his stitches are. He made me willow bark tea. As soon as I'm healed up, he will teach me how to shoot."

Georgie sighed. "I wish it hadn't become a necessity. I want people to mind their own business. Some people don't seem to understand the war has been over a while now."

"Too bad they can't find these men," Veronica said.

Sondra came in with the teapot and cups. She placed the tray on the table. "Too many people and no jobs. That's the problem. Parker created jobs for the freedmen but now there's been grumbling that those jobs should have gone to white people. I say if you don't like it move along. There is no reason to be shooting at people or putting red ants where the children sit." She sat down in one chair.

Georgie poured the tea and handed the cups around. "I forgot to ask. Glory how did you fair with the ant problem?"

Glory's face heated. "They climbed up my legs before I knew what happened. I've never seen ants like that before. Nasty insects for sure."

"We boiled tons of clothes. I'm afraid your dress didn't come out well," Veronica added.

Glory nodded. "Between blood and ants I'm almost out of dresses. I have the material. I'll just have to wait until I'm able to sew. I cut out the pattern already."

Georgie took a sip of her tea. "Send Kent over with the pieces and I'll sew it for you," Georgie offered.

"No, you have enough to do."

"I'd be happy to. If you don't send Kent here, I'll send Parker there."

Glory laughed. "I'll send him, thank you."

"So, who is the spy? Max is bent on finding out. He's so used to being in the Army where men watch each other's back he's fit to be tied. He immediately ruled out anyone who was in the Army." Veronica said.

"There are some new men I'm not familiar with. I knew just about everyone at one time," Georgie told them.

"Could be a woman," Sondra commented.

"The school and my teaching seemed to spark it off. I almost decided it wasn't worth it but that is what they want. It's made me more determined to teach."

Georgie nodded. "It'll be just a few more days before everyone helps to build the school. All the wives are bringing a dish to pass."

"I'm making a few pies," Veronica said before she drank some tea.

"I won't be able to bring anything unless Kent makes it." Glory's stomach clenched. She wanted to do her part.

The three women laughed. "It's fine, Glory no one expects you to bring anything."

Just then the children started fighting. They all wanted a certain block that Bridey had.

"I'd best get Teddy home for a nap. Those blocks look the same."

"To me too," Veronica agreed.

"They are the same. It's definitely naptime," Georgie chuckled.

They gathered the children and said their goodbyes.

It surprised Glory to see the ranch hand, Monty, sitting on chair on her porch. He always had a scraggly unwashed look about him though he didn't smell bad. He stood as they approached.

"Kent sent me to watch the house, Mrs. Sandler." He hurried down the steps and took Teddy. "You shouldn't be lifting. That's what Kent said. I'll be right outside and if you hear someone walking around the house that would be me. Kent said if anything happened…" He turned red. "You'll be safe with me Ma'am."

"Thank you, Monty and please call me Glory. I'll need you to carry Teddy into the house for me." She went inside first while Monty followed her.

"they have ordered two windows for your house, Glory." Monty put Teddy down near his blocks.

"Oh, thank you for letting me know, Monty."

He beamed. "I'll be right outside if needed. Don't forget to lock the door behind me."

She walked him to the door and locked it behind him. Though needed it was a strange thing to have a guard. She was thankful that she hadn't been in Texas during the Civil War. Many things had been rationed up north but down here they'd probably suffered a great deal.

Teddy sat there and examined each block until he found one he liked. It looked the same to her but according to the little ones they were all different.

"I'll get you some milk, Teddy."

He barely looked up from his block. When he took his nap she would examine all the blocks.

She went into the kitchen and easily poured the milk into a tin cup. Then she carried it to Teddy and held it to his lips as he drank it. She wanted to laugh; his eyes were drooping.

"How about a nice nap?"

"No nap." Teddy said as he yawned.

"Let's lay on the bed then. Come on." She walked into the bedroom hoping he'd follow her and he did. Her shoulder was sore as she lifted him onto the bed.

"Mama, too." His bright blue eyes pulled her in, and she napped right beside him.

KENT LOOKED at the letter one cowboy had given him. The cowboy was given it in town the night before and it had Glory's name on it. No postage had been stamped on it. It must be from someone in town.

He nodded to Monty and knocked on the door. A short time later Glory opened it. Her hair practically stood on end. Kent walked in, his lips twitching. It wouldn't be right to laugh at her. He looked at her again and quickly glanced away. He was going to laugh. He couldn't help stare at her and the rumbling began in his chest and resulted into a long laugh. He tried to stop a few times and failed. Finally, the anger on her face settled him.

"A letter came for you." He bit his bottom lip to keep all laughter at bay. He handed the letter to her and watched as she examined the envelope.

"Who do you think it's from?"

"The only way to find out is to open it." He grinned, and it earned him the evil eye glare.

Glory sat on the sofa, opened it and read it. She smiled. "Someone has found Manor, but no one seems to remember seeing James. Lucy was right they went by the last name Roebuck. Manor is now with Adelle and waiting for someone to come get him."

"That's great news! It was worth asking about the boys. We must arrange a way to get him out here. The wagon would just be a target if we don't hide him. Did you want to tell Lucy?"

"Yes, Teddy is sleeping. We went to tea at Georgie's today. It was nice to talk to women again." Glory stood smoothed down her dress. "I will see Lucy now."

"Are you sure you want to go now?" He tried to keep a straight face.

"Out with it. What's so funny?"

"Your hair is sticking on end and it has a piece of peppermint candy in it."

Her hand flew to her hair and her eyes grew wide. "How did Teddy get a piece of candy?"

"I gave him a piece last night. He must have left it on the bed somehow."

"I made the bed this morning, and I didn't see it. My hair is sticky. I'll attract bees!"

Kent laughed. "We'll just put water on that part of your hair. I'm sure you'll be fine. Here let me help you."

They both walked into the kitchen where Kent took some hot water out of the stove reserve and gently got the piece of candy out of her hair. Then he washed the area that was sticky. Her closeness had a definite effect on him and he longed to take her to bed. Patience was torture.

She smiled at him and her eyes were full of pleasure. It amazed him she had no idea just how beautiful she was. Her dark hair had a pretty shine to it and her blue eyes made him think of the sky on a snowy day.

As soon as he was done he stepped away from her. It wouldn't do to act like a randy schoolboy. "We must wait until Teddy wakes up. You can't go alone."

Her shoulders slumped. "I know it's not your fault but all this violence and security is disheartening. I used to wake up in the dormitory, get ready and have breakfast with all the other girls. Then the school day began. I never really went beyond the walls of the school or orphanage very much. I always felt safe there."

"I'm trying my best."

She turned and went to him, putting her good arm around his middle and her head on his chest. "I'm not blaming you. I'm just frustrated. I should be thankful for all I have instead of complaining." She pulled back and tilted back her head until her gaze met his. "Forgive me?"

He wanted nothing more than to nibble on her delectable mouth but he wouldn't be able to stop and her first time deserved to more than taking her on the sofa. "There's nothing to forgive. Granted, it's been a hard time lately but it'll change, eventually. We must show our strength so no one will dare to tangle with anyone on this ranch. So far they've caught us unaware but now we're waiting."

"Can Monty escort me to Lucy's? I'm dying to tell her the news."

He smiled and kissed her forehead. "That's an excellent idea."

CHAPTER ELEVEN

*M*onty wasn't much of a talker. He walked with Glory with nary a word said. Glory was too excited to care. This time when she walked into Joy no one went inside their house. It was a nice feeling. She went directly to Lucy's house and smiled when she found the woman sitting on the front porch snapping beans.

"Well, howdy Glory. When is school going to start again?" Lucy smiled at her. She gestured for her to sit in the other chair on the porch.

Glory sat down. "I have news for you. Good news. They have found Manor."

"Oh, Lord, thank you! Where is he? Is he all right? Is James with him? How far away are they?"

"Manor is in town and is being taken care of by Adelle. There is no word on James though. I asked Adelle to ask around using the last name Roebuck. The letter was brief and didn't say much more than she had Manor but not James."

Lucy put her hand to her chest and smiled with tears in her eyes. "I never thought I'd lay eyes on either of them ever again. It nearly broke me when they took them away. It happened often on the plantation. Being with child was a scary time. You still had to work as hard and you didn't know if you'd be raising the child or not. But having children was encouraged. I guess so they could sell the children for more than cotton."

Glory gasped. She'd never thought of it that way. "Your life has been so hard and I'm sorry."

Lucy reached out and took Glory's hand. "You're one of the angels. Never forget that. When do I get my Manor? Anthony will want to go get his son right away."

"Kent and Parker will work out the details. They want to sneak him here. There's too much trouble on the roads for all those who aren't white."

Lucy nodded. "It don't surprise me. Adelle is a good woman and Liberty Town is safe for Manor. How's your shoulder? Did you put something on your ant bites?"

"I'm healing just fine. If I hear anything else, I'll tell you. Tell no one else. Someone has been giving information to the Pale-Faces. They knew everything we were going to do before we did it." She gave Lucy's hand a quick squeeze before she stood.

"Saturday we will build the schoolhouse right where the first one was. I hope to see you there," Glory said loud enough for her neighbors to hear.

"I understand. We'll be there to help. Thank you for stopping by."

"My pleasure," Glory said before she walked away. Monty was right behind her. There was silence again. "Monty, do you have family near here?"

His eyes widened. It appeared he didn't expect her to speak. "No, Ma'am."

"Have you lived in Texas long?"

"I'm the last of my family and we've been here since

before the Alamo. We had a nice piece of land but the government took it from me. Generations of my family fought and died for that land and just like it's not mine anymore."

"Why did they take it?"

He shrugged. "Once they freed all the slaves, I was hard put to get a crop in. I tried all the tricks. I told them they weren't free here in Texas. Then I told them they had to work for me in exchange for a roof over their heads and food in their bellies. Then I made them all apprentices. The government just kept interferin'. Finally, I couldn't pay my taxes so here I am."

He gave her a slight smile, but she saw the bitterness in his eyes. Had any other men who worked on the ranch ex-slave holders? Monty just might be the spy.

They arrived at the house and she thanked Monty and went inside. She smiled when she saw Kent examining each block.

"Let me guess. Teddy has a favorite block and you can't figure out why that one and not another."

"It's terribly puzzling. They are all the same."

"Same thing happened at Georgie. The kids all fought over one of the blocks and we couldn't figure it out either." She laughed.

Teddy stood holding on the table. He was smiling at her and he took a step. He looked delighted with himself until he fell.

She raced to his side and hugged him. "What a big boy you are. I'm so proud of you!"

The expression of pride on Kent's face warmed her heart.

"He's making such strides. Teddy, you are the best boy!"

Teddy smiled. "Eat," he said with a smile.

"I'll put grub on. I can't wait until you're healed, honey.

I'm tired of my cooking." He got up and walked to the kitchen.

Her stomach dropped. She needed to do something about her lack of cooking skills and fast. Maybe Veronica could help her.

"Oh, Lucy is excited, and she wanted to know when she could have her son."

Kent turned from the table where he was chopping vegetables. "Tonight," he whispered. It was just loud enough for her to hear him.

She instantly felt worried. "Why go to town tonight? Won't it be dangerous?"

With a jerk of his head he indicated that she should go to him. She went to the kitchen and sat at the table.

"I will pretend that we're having a fight and I'm going to the saloon and Willis will go too."

"I don't like that idea," she said frowning.

"Why not?" he whispered.

"It'll shame me to have people think you'd rather be with one of those women and not me," she whispered.

"Aw honey, I'm going to go for a drink is all. No one will think the other."

She doubted he was right, but she wanted Manor home as much as she did.

"It's the only way I could think of to smuggle Manor onto the ranch. You know those hooded men would rather string him up. Willis already told Letty to spread the word that everyone has to act natural and when they see Manor, to act as though he's always been here. It'll be safer all around."

She nodded. "Letty will make sure Lucy and Anthony sit tight. You have enough on your mind without me objecting. I'm sorry."

Before she knew it she was in Kent's arms and he was kissing her deeply. Her shoulder hurt but it was worth it. It was a tender yet yearning kiss, and she wished they could explore each other more. The kiss ended too soon and Kent lifted Teddy up so he could give her a kiss too.

She'd been selfish thinking about herself. Poor Lucy has been without her child for too long. "Is something burning?" she teased.

"Seeing as I haven't cooked yet I don't see how anything could be burning." He grinned at her and put Teddy down. He then continued to chop the vegetables.

"How is your shoulder today?"

"I haven't pulled the stitches out, so I'd say good."

He shook his head. "Just the same, I'll look at it later."

He really cared about her, she could tell. She'd heard the expression of having a song in your heart. She finally knew what it meant.

"Could you help me down to the floor so I can play with Teddy?"

Kent wiped his hands on a towel. "Sure thing. Careful playing blocks. You might try to play with the one that's the favorite."

She chuckled at Kent's teasing. He was gentle as he set her on the floor. "Thank you."

"You are welcome my sweet."

Teddy toddled over to her. "Sweet."

"That's right, Teddy. Your mother is sweet."

Her face heated. She couldn't recall ever being called sweet before. Teddy sat next to her and stacked the blocks. Glory tried to help, but he didn't want her to play with him. He stacked them in a haphazard way saving one block for the top. The special block she suspected was the one he put on top.

"No wonder he likes this one the best," she said, proud of her observation skills.

"Well, what's the secret?" Kent asked.

"I will not tell you. You'll have to figure it out for yourself."

Kent tilted his head and stared at her. "So, it's like that is it?"

"Exactly like that." She couldn't help the wide smile that spread across her face.

Kent stared at her some more and then went back to cooking. Glory didn't like having to pretend to fight later. She didn't know how to fight, not really. If there was ever a confrontation, Fae, Harriet or Imogene would fight for her. They'd sheltered her.

"I must write to Madam Wigg soon and ask about Xenia. Certainly the picture I saw on the wanted poster couldn't be her. But on the off chance it is, they should know."

Kent laughed. "I find it hard to believe anyone from your school could be mixed up in train robbing."

"I can't imagine." She went back to playing with Teddy. He loved to be tickled.

It wasn't long before Kent announced it was time to eat. He helped her up and held her chair out for her. Then he lifted Teddy and sat with him on his lap.

"I must leave as soon as I'm done eating. Leave the dishes. I'll get them when I get back." His voice was low, but she heard him.

"What are we going to fight about?"

"I'm going to town with Willis tonight," he announced loudly. He looked at her and nodded indicating it was her turn.

"Why would you need to go to town at night?" She hoped she was loud enough.

"I just am. You don't need a reason."

"I think you're wrong about that." She stuck her tongue out at him.

His lips twitched and she was afraid they'd end up laughing instead of fighting.

"This isn't some all-girls school. Men like to unwind in town. I'm sorry but I'm going whether or not you like it."

"You'd best not come back here smelling of perfume." She jutted her chin out. She meant those words.

Kent finished feeding Teddy and quickly finished his own meal.

"Giving me the silent treatment are you?" He yelled.

Teddy cried.

"If you will go, then go. You're upsetting our son."

Kent kissed Teddy's cheek and put him on Glory's lap. Next he gave Glory a long kiss. "All right, I'm going." He quickly gathered what he needed and shot out the door.

Glory kissed Teddy and tickled him until he laughed again. That wasn't so bad. She'd been afraid they'd have to say horrible things about each other. She couldn't think of anything awful about Kent.

She locked the door and drew the curtains closed. The only window they didn't fix was the bedroom one. It seemed wiser to defend the house if they didn't have to worry about anyone shooting through that window. A chill went through her and she shivered. She prayed that Kent, Willis and Manor would all come home safely.

Long after Teddy was tucked in, the wagon finally pulled up. It drove down to Joy and stayed for a few minutes before heading back to the barn. Glory's heart pounded. It must mean everything went well. The wait for Kent seemed long but as soon as his boots hit the porch she had the door open.

Kent picked her up and kissed her soundly. Then he put her back down and grinned. "By golly not only did we get Manor but James was there as well!"

She widened her eyes and her heart leaped in excitement.

"Oh, Lucy must be in heaven. I'm so glad they were both there!"

"Those two boys are so different. Manor is bright, and he loves to talk while James seems to be afraid of the world. I'm hoping when he really realizes he is safe here it'll help him."

Kent pulled her close. His chest was so hard and she leaned against it she felt safe and loved. A jolt went through her. She really loved him. The way he ran his big hands up and down her back made her sigh. There was no place on earth she'd rather be.

Kent pulled back as she sighed and put a finger under her chin to lift it. Then he lowered his head staring into her eyes before he took her lips. There was something in his eyes and she hoped it was love. Readily she opened her mouth to him as he deepened the kiss.

"Your shoulder," he whispered as he took his lips from hers.

"It's fine."

He kept his arms around her but stepped back. "It would be best to wait."

Disappointment washed over her and she wanted to protest but she didn't want to seem too forward. She simply nodded. He made her feel things she'd never felt before. Feelings she never knew about before. As long as he loved her she could wait.

He let go of her and pulled a necklace out of his pocket. "This was my mother's. She wore it as far back as I can remember. I'd like you to have it."

It was a silver heart locket with intricate etching on it. "It's beautiful. I'm surprised you didn't give it to your first wife." He put it around her neck and she fingered it as she smiled.

"She would have pawned it the minute I turned my back. This necklace meant too much and I couldn't bring myself to allow her to have it. She knew about it and was furious." He smiled at her. "It looks mighty fine around your neck. I've always kept it with me."

"I'm honored that you gave it to me. Thank you. It's beautiful."

He stared into her eyes. "Beautiful is the exact word I was thinking of."

Her face heated in pleasure. He loved her, she could tell. Now to get through the school raising tomorrow and hopefully the violence would stop.

With any luck, the school supplies would arrive soon. Madam Wigg's dream had become hers. It was a very worthy endeavor. She was always for educating the less fortunate. She might have changed the face of the west. Imagine, twenty-six teachers sent out west as teachers. It was a big legacy for Madam Wigg.

"I supposed it's bedtime," Kent said, interrupting her musing.

"Yes! We have so much to do tomorrow."

"Don't hurt your shoulder again." He took her hands in his. "I want to make our marriage real as soon as you're able."

She bit her bottom lip as she nodded. "Me too."

CHAPTER TWELVE

*T*he sound of hammering started early the next morning. Kent was eager to get out there to help but Glory insisted they have breakfast first. After he rustled up eggs and bread, they were soon on their way.

Teddy laughed and clapped in excitement and at the last minute he grabbed his favorite block. What was the secret of the block?

Someone set tables and benches up under one of the biggest trees around while men hammered and sawed. It was strange to see both black and white people working together. It was nice.

"I wish I had brought a dish to pass," Glory said.

"Next time," Kent replied. "I want you sitting and resting today."

"Yes, Kent," she replied as she smiled at him. "I believe my shoulder is feeling better every day."

She probably meant to tease him but she was the one who ended up with a red face.

"It looks as though everyone is here," she observed.

"Yes, and many you can't see. If anything happens, push the tables over on their sides and take cover."

"I'll keep an eye out."

"That's my girl."

A look of doubt crossed her face. "Am I your girl?"

"You sure are." He helped her to the tables and set Teddy on the ground near her. Then he bent and kissed her on the mouth in front of everyone. He was still chuckling about the look of surprise and embarrassment she wore.

He picked up a hammer and was soon helping to build the school. With so many people there and Parker taking the lead, it didn't take more than half a day to get it finished. Kent kept expecting trouble but maybe the Pale-Faces didn't want to be out in the daylight. He enjoyed the happiness on Glory's face as she talked with the other women and then turned constantly to check on the progress.

Kent put down the hammer and walked to her. "Veronica could you watch Teddy for a bit?"

"I'd be happy to."

Kent took Glory's hand and escorted her to the school.

"I didn't think it would be so spacious," she said.

"It'll be used for church services and meetings too." The smell of fresh wood hit them as they walked inside.

Her jaw dropped. "There are tables and chairs!"

"One man had been working on them for a while now."

He took pride in the way she ran her hands over her desk. "I made that."

She turned and stared at him. "On my, it's so beautiful. Now if only the supplies would get here. Thank you so much, Kent."

He led her outside and took her to a wagon that was covered with white canvas. A few of the hands took the canvas off and Glory's jaw dropped. "All the supplies I asked for are in the wagon. How did they get here so fast? There are books and slates and chalk. Paper and pencils and even a quill pen with a bottle of ink." Tears filled her eyes. "I miss the school and orphanage and all the girls and especially Madam Wigg.

"Here's the letter that came with the supplies." Kent handed it to her and watched as she read it.

"It's a letter of encouragement, telling me how proud of me she is. She asked if I had seen Xenia in these parts. Do you think I should tell her about the wanted poster?"

"You don't know for certain it's your friend on that poster. I wouldn't upset the older woman just yet."

Glory nodded. "You're right. Let's get everything moved into the school." She reached for a pile of books but Kent swung her up in his arms.

He walked to the rest of the women. "Make sure she stays put. Her shoulder still isn't healed."

"Don't you worry, Kent," Georgie said. "We'll keep an eye on her."

"I appreciated it." He tipped his hat to all the ladies before he headed to the wagon with the supplies in it. He helped to unload it and then he stood back and admired the school.

Parker walked toward him and gave him a friendly slap on the back. "Looks good."

"It sure does."

"Don't you worry; I found a whole group of ex-soldiers without jobs. They will guard the ranch and the school."

"That's a relief."

"Kent," Georgie said as she hurried toward him. "Can I speak to you?"

He furrowed his brow. "Of course you can."

"You know I was going to take the pieces of fabric that Glory had cut and sew it for her. I will have to make some drastic changes."

"Why?"

"One sleeve is six inches longer than the other. If I didn't know better, I'd say a drinking woman had cut out the pattern. Unless I shorten the hem quite a bit the bottom won't look right. Part of the hem is much shorter than the other."

"I thought the school taught her to sew?"

"We'll if they did she didn't pay attention. If you could get other fabric to me I'll make her one. And Kent, I'm not trying to stir up trouble. Actually, I want to do the opposite. Glory can only make cookies and bread. I let her borrow my cook book so encourage her."

Parker snorted. "Kent, I have a feeling you'll be losing weight."

He chuckled. "I think she mentioned she had a private place within the school where she would read. Maybe it was during sewing and cooking classes."

Parker roared louder. "She tries," he finally could get out.

"That she does. Let's go eat," Georgie suggested.

Kent's lips were twitching. "Might be the last good meal I get for a while."

A few days later Glory went from being ecstatic to being so frustrated she wanted to cry. They decided that school would start next week. Every day she'd set things up and daydreamed. She had to admit she was a good teacher. Her approach was a combination of nurturing and being firm when she had to.

She envisioned her students watching her with eagerness. She was giving them a precious gift. The gift of reading. They hadn't figured out the adult classes yet but it would all fall into place. She glanced out the window. Monty had taken his post outside of the school guarding her and Teddy.

Teddy walked along the benches. He held on and went all around the room. Hid face lit up when she told him how proud of him she was. There was an area in a corner that was sectioned off. This was for Teddy while she taught. It was big enough for him to play and a small bed for naps and such.

It was a brilliant idea and Kent let her know daily it was his suggestion. Some towns only wanted unmarried women for teachers but this community was different. She'd been invited down to Joy every day so far. Meeting Manor and James for the first time brought tears to her eyes. The poor boys seemed bewildered. Neither could sit still but that was probably expected being uprooted repeatedly. She met with different families and had tea with the mother while she got to know the students. She already had an idea from when she taught them under the tree but this was a real school.

Some of their stories were heartbreaking. Many still had missing family members. How could a person honestly believe they could own another person? She tried to understand it from the slave owners view point but she couldn't imagine it. Parker and Georgie had been so generous to everyone. From the jobs he gave to the men who served under his command to people who couldn't afford to feed their families to the freemen who now lived in Joy.

It gave her a happy sense of purpose to know she was being of help too. She had a new dress to wear for her first day. Georgie had somehow burned part of the fabric to the dress that had been ready to sew so she came back for more material and the dress was perfect. It was green her favorite color. She'd have to ask Georgie to teach her to sew, but she'd wait until after school started. Her shoulder was on the mend.

Cooking would be a disaster, and she dreaded it. Helping Kent in the kitchen was teaching her a few skills. He liked to talk about cooking and the reason he did everything. There was never a moment of silence. She'd have to tell him the awful truth and it would probably have to be tonight. Well, maybe not. She could try to cook. She'd read the cookbook three times. She was probably good to go.

"Mama," Teddy called pointing out the window.

She went to the window and quickly stepped back so she wasn't seen. Monty was talking with men she didn't know. Her stomach dropped as she grabbed her pistol out of her bag. She wasn't a good shot yet, but she suspected that when her shoulder was completely healed, she'd be much better. Kent hoped that the threat of a gun would keep danger at bay. And he's trusted Monty.

The men kept glancing at the school and she didn't like the gleam she saw in their eyes. Then they all laughed and left. Monty stood where he had been. Kent trusted Monty, so had she. Should she confront him or wait? Waiting could be a death sentence but a confrontation was bound to get them hurt or worse.

They wouldn't go straight home she decided. Kent was at the corral and she needed to tell him. She saw Monty coming close to the window, and she pretended to dust the tables. He tapped on the window and her heart skipped a beat. She smiled and waved.

Next she got their belongings together and with the pistol in her pocket she carried Teddy out of the school. She took her time locking the door, needing to compose herself. By the time she was done she felt more in control.

"We will meet Kent at the corral. Teddy wants to see the horses."

"See horses!" Teddy said in glee.

Monty didn't look pleased.

"Plus, it'll give you a break. It must be boring watching over me and sweet little Teddy. I bet you'd rather be with the cattle."

His eyes widened as if surprised. "Yes, getting back to the cattle will come soon enough." He didn't say another word. He led them to the barn and kept walking.

She carried Teddy to the corral and was warmed straight through by Kent's smile. His smiles and his eyes had been making promises to her she wasn't certain of but thought she'd like them.

"My favorite family," he said as he kissed her cheek and then Teddy's. "Not ready to go inside yet?"

"You know how much Teddy loves to watch you with the horses." She smiled and leaned into him. "I think Monty is the spy," she whispered while she still smiled.

Kent stared at her for a moment. "Here give Teddy so he can pet the horses." After he had Teddy in his arms, he led them to the opposite side of the corral. "What are you talking about?" His voice was low.

"Which one do you like the best, Teddy?" She leaned and put her head against Kent's arm. "He had some meeting in front of the school."

He gave her a look of alarm. "What?"

"There were four men who didn't belong on the ranch talking and laughing with him. They kept glancing at the school."

"Your gun?"

"In my pocket."

Kent smiled. "Good." Kent took Teddy's hand and showed him how to pet the horse nicely. "You know, Veronica asked if you could stop by her place. Willis is there now so we might as well go."

"Here let me hold Teddy." She took him into her arm. Kent would need his hands free if trouble started.

They walked to the Sandler house and were welcomed inside. Glory sat Teddy on the floor near Bridey. Her hands shook as she rejoined the other three adults. She stood in the circle of Kent's safe arms while he retold her story.

Max ran his fingers through his dark hair. "No need to worry. Monty is one of us. We hired him to ferret out the spy. He must have made headway if those men will meet with him."

Veronica stared at her husband. "You could have told me at least."

Max shook his head. The more people that know something just means the better the chance someone will slip up and say something they shouldn't have. Parker and I were the only ones who knew. Sorry you got left out of the loop, Kent."

"You're right. It's best to keep it quiet. So what do we do now?" Kent leaned his cheek against the top of Glory's head.

"Act natural?" Max grinned. He glanced at his wife. "Veronica might have to stay inside until this is over. She doesn't have a poker face."

Veronica hit him in the side with her elbow.

"They'll probably strike as soon as today. I have a feeling who the spy is. We'll need Walter, Willis and Parker and Monty on it." I think it best if everyone holed up at Parker's place. He has plenty of rifles and we've defended the place before. We will need men inside the school too."

"How are you going to get them there without being seen?" Glory asked.

"Good question," Max said.

"We use the shipping crates all the school supplies came in. We can fit a man in each and have others waiting nearby." Kent pulled Glory closer to him. "Let's get you women and the kids to Georgie's. Veronica you might as well pack a bag. They'll think it's baby stuff."

Veronica nodded. "Her stuff takes up a whole bag. I'll put

extra nappies for Teddy." She turned and walked into the bedroom. Her face was pale probably from fear.

Monty was in on it? They fooled her or rather he did. He seemed like a slacker who didn't know too much. You can never tell about people. What she really knew about the Southwest and its people could fill a thimble. Sondra would probably cook dinner that would save Glory her fated truth telling for another night.

Kent escorted them to Parker's and she didn't want to let him go. He handed Teddy to Georgie and took Glory out onto the front porch.

"You'll be fine." He stared into her eyes.

"It's not me I'm frightened for. I can't lose you." Her emotions jumbled.

"It is getting a bit cold. Who would keep the firewood full?" he teased.

It surprised her that a tear rolled down her face. "It's not about firewood. It's…" She glanced away trying to compose herself.

Kent cupped her chin in his hand and turned her head until she was looking at him. "Glory what's wrong? I don't think I've ever seen you like this. You're the gal who stitched herself up." His smile was soft and gentle.

"This is worse, much worse. I think I've fallen in love with you. I don't see how I could have."

His brow furrowed. "Is there something about me that leads you to believe loving me would be so awful?"

She blinked. "Awful? No, not at all. It's just how can I know I love you if we haven't." she glanced over her shoulder. "I, we haven't had relations."

His lips twitched. "Relations, I see. Glory, look at me. Relations are much better when you love the person you're with. I'm so honored you love me because I love you. I have from the very first time you took Teddy into your arms and treated him as your own. Love is a good thing." He bent until his lips were on hers.

His kiss put the emotional fire out while it kindled a raging fire of love and desire. She gasped as he deepened the kiss and pulled her against him. She felt his evidence of desire and stilled. Then she broke off the kiss and stared at him.

"That's just the way a man's body reacts when he's kissing the woman he loves. I have to go and don't you worry, I'll be filling the wood bin soon."

Her face felt hot. Just how red was she? "Be careful."

Kent kissed her again and hugged her tight. "You too." He let her go and headed to the barn. When he got there, he turned and smiled at her before he went inside.

"Glory," Georgie called. "The tea is ready."

Glory took a deep steadying breath and walked inside.

CHAPTER THIRTEEN

*K*ent, Parker, Max and Willis all walked toward the homestead with their horses walking beside them. It had been some hard riding, and the horses needed a break. They were silent for a long while as the moonlight showed them the path.

"Max, feeling light-headed yet?" Parker asked.

"The bleeding isn't so bad. Veronica will patch me up good as new."

"We hadn't had to fight like that in years," Parker commented.

"We came through it like we always do," Kent said. "Willis, you all right?"

"I am. I was just thinking I have no one to patch me up."

"Willis, where did you get hit?" Max asked.

"I didn't but it would be good to have someone waiting for me. With the three of you being married things aren't the same."

"Get yourself a wife and I'll have a house built for you," Parker offered.

"That's the thing. I don't think I'm the one woman type."

Max laughed. "You find the right woman and you'll be surprised how you change."

"How are things going with you and Glory, Kent?" Willis asked.

"Slow but good. I need a favor. Glory and I haven't, well we haven't consummated the marriage." He knew they would laugh. "Laughter? What about helping a man out?"

"Kent, I think we need to talk," Parker started. "It's a one man type of thing."

Kent pretended he didn't hear Parker. He didn't want to disrespect his wife with anymore jokes. "I need someone to take Teddy for the night."

"Leave him at the house with Georgie and me. He'll probably be sleeping, anyway."

"I'd appreciate it, Parker."

"Always glad to help," he started out on an even footing but he ended up laughing. "I'm sorry. You and Glory are a great match."

"I'm surprised the Yankees came to our aid. I thought they had no trouble with the Pale-Faces." Max commented.

"They probably just wanted to know who those hooded men were. They rode their own horses and wore their own boots. It wasn't too hard to figure out who was under those white hoods." Kent said.

Willis nodded. "I wanted to call out a few of them when I was in town but I had no proof. But now we do."

"It's the Army's problem now," Parker said. "There's Crumb. Just play along."

They walked a bit more until they were at the barn. Crumb took a step forward. "I'll take care of your horses. What happened?"

"All the Pale-Faces are dead. They mentioned a spy among us. Can you imagine such a thing?" Parker calmly said.

Crumb turned white. "They are all dead? What about my broth–" He clamped his hand over his mouth.

Parker took a step forward and took Crumb's gun from his holster. "Get off my land. I ever see you again and it'll be shoot first and ask questions later. Got it?"

Crumb turned and ran into the woods. It was a relief to see him gone. Now Glory wouldn't have to worry. A few hands poured out of the bunkhouse and took the reins from the men. They were free to go into the house.

They hardly took a step before the door flew open and Georgie, Veronica and Glory ran out.

"See what I mean?" Willis whispered.

Kent didn't care about Willis' plight. He only had eyes for his wife. She was handful enough for him and he had plans for her.

He scooped her up and carried her to their house. She asked about Teddy but he silenced her with a kiss. He set her down in the main room suddenly as nervous as a green boy. He'd been married but somehow this was different. Glory was different. How much love he felt was different too.

"Is something wrong?" she asked hesitantly.

He took her small hand into his. She deserved better than him. "It's just that if we do this, you can't change your mind and leave."

Glory snatched her hand back and put her hands on her hips. "Have I asked to leave? Have I tried to sneak away? Have I given you any indication I wasn't happy here? You need not answer because it is not. I love Teddy as if he were mine. In fact, he is mine. I yearn for you and I love you to distraction but if you're the one having doubts, tell me now." She lifted her chin as if daring him to contradict her.

He loved the way her blue eyes flashed when she was mad. Reaching behind her head, he took out her hairpins. He'd barely seen it down. By the time she was ready for bed she had it braided. Her dark tresses fell down her back in waves. He put his hand on some and brought it forward to hang down the front of her.

"You're so lovely. When you agreed to be my bride, I hoped and prayed I'd get a kind, loving woman and I did. I want to make you mine, really mine." His voice grew husky.

"I'm nervous too." She took a step forward, and he put his arms around her. "I do love you and I want everything that comes with being married. I heard it's best if you love the person." She gave him a teasing smile.

He gave her his most tender kiss, and it had never been so sweet. He deepened it and she whimpered in a good way. She enjoyed his attentions. He took a deep breath and scooped her up into his arms. He'd make it beautiful for her he vowed.

GLORY'S EYES FLUTTERED OPEN, and she automatically smiled. Then she remembered the night before and pressed her hand over her heart. Kent wasn't in bed with her. She grabbed a shawl and wrapped it around herself before she went padding out of the bedroom.

What if he hadn't felt the wonder of last night the same way she did? Her face heated as she remembered his gentleness at the beginning and his urgency toward the end. She continued into the kitchen and Kent was making breakfast. Guilt about her little cooking lie hit her.

Kent took a pan off the cook stove. Her quickly gathered her up into his arms and gave her a long leisurely, loving kiss. "How's my beautiful wife this morning?"

Embarrassed she hid her face against his neck.

He hugged her tight and then when he let go he took a step back. "Last night made me feel in awe. I was right it is so much better when you're with the person you love. You, my wife, are a passionate woman and I'm glad for it. Now, let's eat and get our son."

She nodded. She'd felt in awe too. She never knew, but the wait was well worth it. He loves her, and she didn't need to hide behind anyone when she was with him.

"I need to confess something to you."

He turned to her and his lips twitched.

She narrowed her eyes. "You already know! Did Georgie tell you?" She sighed. "It doesn't matter, it's true. I can't cook. I can make bread and cookies but other than some porridge I'm a disaster. I know you expected a wife who could cook." She stared at the floor.

"Hey, it's not so bad. You're a heck of a smart woman. You can learn and I'll try to be understanding."

"Try?"

"I might not be able to eat everything you make. I'm just covering the possibilities." He chuckled.

"Fair enough." She smiled at her handsome husband. God looked her way when husbands were chosen. Hopefully, all of her friends were experiencing the same.

EPILOGUE

*G*lory stood at the front of the classroom taking in all the happy eager faces. She wished Madam Wigg could see her now. She'd be proud. Each child had a reading primer and a slate in front of them.

If not for her, Glory wasn't sure that the children would have ever gotten an education. There were men outside guarding the school and they would walk the children home. She glanced at Teddy who happily played in his little area. Kent would come after school to take them home.

Crumb had been arrested as well as the rest of the Pale-Faces but there had been no justice. They were freed within a few days. It wasn't against the law to wear white hoods and no one who was hurt could identify the men but everyone knew who they were.

It had appalled her that so many people didn't care. The freedmen would have a long road to travel to really be free. She was determined to unite more families. It was the right thing to do. She still could not understand the mindset of so many people in the South and she never would.

Glory smoothed down her new dress. Georgie had

brought it to her yesterday as a surprise. Georgie had explained to Glory about cutting out patterns so one sleeve wasn't longer than the other. At first Glory was embarrassed, but they ended up having a great laugh over it. It was so good to have friends again.

Last evening before supper Parker, Georgie, Max and Veronica showed up at her and Kent's home. They wanted to know the secret of the blocks. The men each held the special block in their hand. Kent had picked up Teddy's favorite too. It was hard to see but there were tiny teeth marks. The block Parker held had three sets of marks on them. The one Max held had two and the one Kent had one but it was deeper. Teddy had more teeth.

They all looked stumped. The Kent wanted to know why they picked that one block to chew on. She didn't have an answer for that.

Glory instructed the class to open their primers. Kent was making Teddy a bed of his own today. They'd decided he could have a room to himself. They wanted their privacy.

Glory went from student to student helping them to form the letter A on their slates. She'd gotten word from Madam Wigg. She thanked Glory for the information about the wanted poster. Xenia had yet to show up. Glory's friends were all fine.

She saw a hand being raised. "Yes, Andrew?"

Andrew stood. "My name starts with A don't it?"

Glory smiled. "Yes, Andrew your name starts with an A and it's doesn't it not don't it."

"Miss Glory I hate to tell you this but we all say don't. We don't use that other word. Are you sure you're right?"

Glory tried not to laugh. "The correct word is doesn't. I'll be teaching you the correct way so when you go out into the world you'll sound well educated."

She would enjoy her life here in Texas.

THE END

I'm so pleased you chose to read Glory's Groom, and it's my sincere hope that you enjoyed the story. I would appreciate if you'd consider posting a review. This can help an author tremendously in obtaining a readership. My many thanks. ~ Kathleen

ABOUT THE AUTHOR

Sexy Cowboys and the Women Who Love Them...
Finalist in the 2012 and 2015 RONE Awards.
Top Pick, Five Star Series from the Romance Review.
Kathleen Ball writes contemporary and historical western
romance with great emotion and
memorable characters. Her books are award winners and
have appeared on best sellers lists including: Amazon's Best
Seller's List, All Romance Ebooks, Bookstrand, Desert
Breeze Publishing and Secret Cravings Publishing Best
Sellers list. She is the recipient of eight Editor's Choice
Awards, and The Readers' Choice Award for Ryelee's
Cowboy.
Winner of the Lear diamond award Best Historical Novel-
Cinders' Bride
There's something about a cowboy

facebook.com/kathleenballwesternromance

twitter.com/kballauthor

instagram.com/author_kathleenball

OTHER BOOKS BY KATHLEEN

Lasso Spring Series

Callie's Heart

Lone Star Joy

Stetson's Storm

Dawson Ranch Series

Texas Haven

Ryelee's Cowboy

Cowboy Season Series

Summer's Desire

Autumn's Hope

Winter's Embrace

Spring's Delight

Mail Order Brides of Texas

Cinder's Bride

Keegan's Bride

Shane's Bride

Tramp's Bride

Poor Boy's Christmas

Oregon Trail Dreamin'

We've Only Just Begun

A Lifetime to Share

A Love Worth Searching For

So Many Roads to Choose

The Settlers

Greg

Juan

Scarlett

Mail Order Brides of Spring Water

Tattered Hearts

Shattered Trust

Glory's Groom

Battered Soul

The Greatest Gift

Love So Deep

Luke's Fate

Whispered Love

Love Before Midnight

I'm Forever Yours

Finn's Fortune

Glory's Groom

47849924R00100

Made in the USA
Lexington, KY
12 August 2019